HEDYLUS

HD

BLACK SWAN BOOKS

Published by
BLACK SWAN BOOKS LTD.
P. O. BOX 327
REDDING RIDGE, CT 06876

ISBN 0-933806-00-0

CONTENTS

To Perdita

HEDYLUS

The wild field-flowers of Hedylus and
Posidippus with Sikeledes' anemones.
The Garland of Meleager

I

HEDYLE OF ATHENS let go the polished mirror. She said, "eyes, nose, mouth. I've seen them all so often. Everybody has an eye—eyes, I mean,—nose, mouth. I am just like all the others." She ran her incredibly slender index along the back of the mirror and her finger told her of curved line of exquisite symmetry, of tenuous curled vine-tendril and somewhere (she felt for it) the slightly too heavily incised, frankly rampant grape-bunch.

"This mirror is like me, inconsistent in particulars. I've been here too long to believe in beauty. Beauty went when the Macedonians undermined our earth works. Sometimes, it's almost too pitiful to watch them at it, all these semi-Asiatic barbarians trying to play at beauty. If Douris weren't so frankly entertaining, I would leave him." Hedyle had said this, thought this every time she looked at herself, every time she lifted a polished mirror.

"I've been here a long time. Only there is no time. I mean, there isn't really. Plato and the peripatetics (though Socrates was an ill-informed monster) had some idea of the nonsense of it, of time's irrelevancy. That's why it doesn't matter." Nevertheless she added an additional grain of fresh kohl to the paste she habitually affected. It doesn't do to appear haggard at assemblies.

7

"I'll never look in a mirror again," she said. "I've done it for too many long years. I used to be so exquisite. Now, I am merely beautiful. It's rather restful just giving up. I mean it's been so amusing, everything. Once you let go the mind and the disastrous spinning of the intellect, everything comes clear. It was the intellect undid me. If I hadn't had a mind, I'd have married the first grain-merchant who approached me. Papa was so fantastic. He believed in the new-fangled curve and line. He believed with the ultra-moderns, of ships starting and coming back to where they sailed from. They never did. All the ships we watched perished in mid-ocean. The Mediterranean is a treacherous water. It all dates back to Philip. Philip of Macedon opened the world too freely. India. Those Scythian marches. The mind in Athens held supreme sway. Philip taught us that the mind was nothing, for ships and ignorant mariners could disprove it. Philip of Macedon undermined the intellectual integrity, as well as the mere material fortresses of Athens."

Hedyle of Athens remained Hedyle, incontrovertibly of Athens. It was all very well for Douris the island's tyrant, to produce her draped in the latest Tyrio-Sidonian purple. Red and red. Grape-red and red of the inner phosphorescent gaping gills of sea-fish. There was no red, no hyacinth-purple that the ornate semi-Asiatic did not find her. "I want you to match the flowers along your terraces."

Hedyle of Athens had accepted her predicament; a transplanted blossom. Yet there wasn't any red or blue or sea-red or sea-blue or deep-ocean purple could outblazon Hedyle, could undermine the marble thing beneath her. She had (a moment since) let go the silver mirror. "I won't look at myself any longer. I used to be so exquisite. Now," her words contradicted her, "I am merely beautiful."

There were a number of things one could do. That new cream, for instance, and steaming; breathing in deep steam from flat bowls and the Egyptian lotion applied afterwards. Hedyle had found the cream soft to her face but acclaimed to the fashionable ladies of the court of Douris that it left the white skin muddy. "These Ethiopians know how to keep away wrinkles, little creeping crow's-feet. But it isn't much good for our purposes." A slave was forced to return to an Alexandrian trading-ship to be lashed by an irate master. The ladies of Samos, it appeared, wouldn't have his offering. He sailed on with his merchandise to Cos. Samos wasn't easily seduced by charlatans. "We must have our parties later," Hedyle humorously asserted.

Hedyle was humorous on these occasions. It was part of her stock in trade. "To be witty, to be humorous," she herself asserted, "distracts attention from insistent crow's-feet." She rather overdid this insistence on shadows that were hardly even shadows, merest spider-webs as it were, woven silver webs softening the (at times) too rigid clarity and coldness of the face outline. Silver. "White hair *can* be attractive," she would remark though she hadn't herself reached the stage of seriously contemplating dyeing. Her own hair still shone incredibly sleek and thick against her small head. She admitted to herself, scanning the mirror for his ravages, that time had dealt easily with Hedyle. "That's because I haven't really cared for Douris." Time, the ravager, left her smiling at her crow's-feet. For what was age? She was younger now than at that season with Demetrius.

Hedyle of Athens lifted her polished mirror. I'll try to escape Demetrius. Something's gone wrong with Samos. I think it's his boat stopping. Demetrius." The word as she pronounced it, brought her superficial casual memory; corridors crowded with banqueters, occasional unexpected shower of rose-leaves and an uplifted naked arm that waved from a stone basin. Demetrius had used his pretended love of beauty to ornament his orgies. His festivals to almost forgotten deities were that, simply. Hedyle of Athens, as a very much younger woman, had been part of that cynical refinement, Athenian decadence. "Not that I ever liked it." She retouched her left eyebrow and ran a finger over her eyelids critically. *"Eye-lids veil—violet petals.* Who wrote of such flower eyelids? It might have been the Mitylenian." Hedyle of Athens still fumbled with her bracelets. "I used to dislike such obvious ornament. It does now to hide deficiencies." She persisted that her body was outworn. It was a minor affectation among others more pretentious.

"I used to dislike bracelets." She tried two, reconsidered, drew them off and found another. It was a metallic ring with a blue stone. "This thing, they told me, came from a lady perished some thousand years before Lycurgus. She was found in an underground sort of temple, wound with grave-cloths. She was easily transported. They wanted me to take her, as she was, as a sort of votive statue. It was desecration. She had been alive once. I said, I wouldn't have her, not on any consideration, neither gift nor barter. The ship that took her away from Samos sank, as I knew it would do, off the Needles. I don't believe in disinterring corpses. A barbaric habit anyway, this wrapping up of live flesh in grave-cloths. Barbaric. If it weren't that the Egyptians were so highly skilled in medicine, it would be indecent. They have, as has always been (even before Herodotus) asserted, skill in balsam, drugs. I always wondered why I kept the bracelet."

She knew why, though she argued round in her mind, her odd insistent manner. The circlet was a narrow band of some unfamiliar metal, gleaming white in daylight, now by lamplight, taking edge of luminous blue. The blue metal was the body of a serpent, merging to frank lapis. The lapis was of a quality rarely found on Samos, yet it was, argue as one would do, at last analysis but lapis. The serpent's head was lapis and he bit his own tail according to convention. His head lay against a blue vein on Hedyle's fore-arm and she had to admit that the Egyptian who invented it, had had an eye to flattery. The great lump just there minimized the arm-breadth and those Egyptians were slim enough already (to judge by that dead lady) in all conscience.

"I wonder if her veins shone blue." The great lapis head exactly matched a blue vein in the Athenian's fore-arm. "Well, there are advantages at Samos. Travel. Seeing and talking. Papa was fantastic. We must never see anybody but the élite and as Athens was a wreck and nobody fit to meet us, we never, logically, saw anyone."

Hedyle of Athens after ten years at Samos, more than fifteen years in all of frank emancipation, still harked back to Athens. "Athens was a stuffy, démodé little hole. How could anyone live in it?"

II

HEDYLE FASTENED HER NECKLET. It clamped with a dynamic little click. She felt the weighted ends of the long threads of gold, heavy against the narrow neck-bones. Curiosity overcame her. She had said she wouldn't look in the mirror but she now did. "After all, the necklet may not go well with the head-band." The head-band was pure silver. "Not everything," she had a thousand times contended against more conventional opinion, "goes with silver." Hedyle's least pronouncements had so long been the last word of fashionable taste on Samos, that she had (she was right in this particular) to look carefully to her laurels.

"The blue of the silver bracelet goes with nothing," she decided, as she held her left fore-arm against the head-band. Then she dropped her braceleted arm in her lap. The Egyptian blue merged subtly with the foreign dress-stuff. "The iridescent over-play of light in this new stuff shows almost purple. The head-band is too clear a silver. There is no use ultimately thinking one can make anything match anything. What was the name of that inventive dame who left everything, sold her mirror, gave it rather, to the Paphian?" Hedyle sought for the familiar lines of Plato, "*I Lais lay my mirror here before your feet* (or something in that manner), *O Paphian.*"

The Paphian? Hedyle had followed her own spirit but not willfully, in sacrificing to the Paphian. What had the Paphian brought her? The eyes of Hedyle, following her half-formed thought, swept the dressing-table. The boxes were over-crowded with pearls, opals, large ornate sapphires. "The table is arrayed," she said, "too negligently." Hedyle added, "old Lyda must be prompted," hardly knowing why she said it. Again vaguely she thought of thieves, inrush of some unknown element. "It must be Demetrius. There are no thieves this end of island Samos." Vaguely she shivered in her iridescent blue. "Something's happened. I feel as I did when old Lyda used to say (when we shivered as young girls, inadvertently) *The Furies walk on your grave.*"

Grave. Hedyle of Athens was too blythe, too cultivated an Athenian to dwell long on such things. She decided it was the bracelet. "That poor slender girl, crowded into a long box painted with water-lilies. I kept the thing because of —superstition." She recalled the crowd gaping and staring and had had Douris send a servant to inquire what new wares had touched at Samos. It was indeed a new commodity. Hedyle had stepped from her litter (she recalled that summer day's particular fall of sunlight) to follow the narrow sea-steps. A face had stared at her; then she lost sight of features brushed in artfully and saw nothing but eyes. Her own eyes stared at her from a narrow box, dropped, as it happened, on their sea-steps, from Alexandria. "I remember how I felt when Douris brought the bracelet and later when they entirely unpacked the thing . . ." She shuddered. "It is impossible." She pulled off the serpent-bracelet.

"Something's gone wrong. Things have been going wrong." Hedyle wondered for the thousandth time with her conscious mind (shutting away this vague disquietude) how her new robes would affect the court-room, for the thousandth time she made the wary statement to herself that she was glad she had kept Douris her so devoted servant. "Marriage in these cases is disastrous." A form shaded the distant doorway. She laid aside the mirror. It was time Lyda came to dress her. Not that she wasn't dressed. It was the tiresome ring of short curls at the neck-nape. She preferred using her own hot irons, though someone had to help her. The touch of the ordinary serving woman exasperated her. But Lyda was different. "Lyda! Hurry with the wraps and over-sandals." Lyda was particular, saw to her keeping well warmed and dry shod this treacherous weather.

Hedyle was glad she had had Lydia keep the braziers burning in the hall-way. There was a pleasant pulse of warmth, just perceptible, not really sullying the cool freshness of the room. Cold and heat in layers, not one stuffy element. She liked it that way. Nevertheless she shivered. "I wish old Lyda'd hurry...this bad weather."

Rains had beaten her in Athens and she hadn't minded. She had followed the processions in all kinds of weather, as a young girl. Always of the mob, but apart, guarded by servants. That was before she knew Demetrius. "Papa was so fantastic." Hedyle recalled a knot of winter violets she had found her father. "I gave him violets, like presenting Zeus with offerings." She had knotted white violets with grass stems. "We never knew our mother." The word, her own thought, answered her in spoken syllable. It spoke from the drawn curtain of the door-way. "Mother."

Hedyle dropped the mirror. Her son entered.

"You speak like a ghost summoned to Hades from a new tomb. What is the matter with you?" She was shuddering in the lamplight. "What *is* the matter, mother?"

"Nothing, Hedylus. You might have the manners (something of Athens in you) to announce yourself more subtly."

"I wasn't aware of any sort of gaucheness."

"Boys grow up so swiftly. You're not a child now."

Hedylus stared astonished at his mother. Face to face in the lamplight, a ghost regarding a painted image from a coffin.

"Are we then so nothing?"

"What do you mean, mama?"

Hedyle stumbled forward. It was so unlike her. "Something's gone wrong with—Samos."

"There's nothing wrong, mama. There are new guests expected. Douris even thought I might look over our old apartment on the other side of Samos. He didn't know who'd take it. He suggested, in order to accommodate the new guests fittingly, he himself might move down here."

Hedyle regarded her child.

"O, Douris. Let him. He can stay here or not as pleases him. I don't care who takes the old winter-pavilion, just so it's not Demetrius."

"Demetrius?"

"You know—the Athenian, delegate to Alexandria. For all, gossip should be disregarded, I can't help feeling that it *is* a sort of exile. Demetrius always had his hand in the wrong sort of politics. He was sure, in spite of his showy reforms, to come to no good."

"Demetrius?"

"Didn't you know? Demetrius of Athens, on his way to Alexandria, stops at Samos."

Hedylus, the son looked at Hedyle, the mother.

"Your old—?"

"Lover—put it frankly. Have I ever concealed anything?" Hedyle of Athens regarded her son with odd disapprobation.

"Haven't I taught you from the first hour of your birth, darling, not to be surprised or not to *show* surprise at anything? Surely you know your—mother."

"I know—Hedyle. But I don't like your odd tone."

"Tone?"

"The way you say it. Your words have an over-emphasis, I don't like. It's not you. You're not pleased to see Demetrius."

"*See* the little monster? Why should I see Demetrius?"

"How can it be avoided?"

"*See* him. Well yes, with Douris. That's hardly seeing, is it?"

"He'll remind you of things—Athens."

"Darling, for some (how many years?) you've been Athens to me."

"Athens but not Athenian."

The boy spoke blithely. It didn't do to talk other than this way. Their conversation now as always was flippant dialogue, snap and spark and exact pause preceding answer. They seemed to count their pauses like trained actors.

It was Hedyle's turn now. She re-arched the delicate line of tenuous eyebrows. That evidently *was* her answer.

Hedylus said, "mama, you put on too much blatant makeup."

She flared, "these things hide wrinkles—the fact that I'm not young." Her very tone of anger was a set thing. She wasn't really angry. She was acting a part, anger was part of acting. Her son wearied her. *He* wasn't really acting, really being witty, when he said, "Athens but not Athenian." Hadn't she all these years tried to make the affair clear to Hedylus? He didn't know his father's name, it's quite true. But neither did Ion, really, neither did young Erechtheus. There was nothing for such as Hedyle and Hedylus but to claim blatant kinship with divinity. The world was no place for them. Knowing that, make the world subservient to you. Douris was that.

"Haven't I told you a thousand times that it's better to be

mysterious in your fore-bears, interesting?" The argument led nowhere. It never had. "I mean, Hedylus nameless, claims a larger heritage than Hedylus, the son of shoddy makeshift politician, merchant, or cheesemonger. What anyhow, is Athens?"

Something had trod on Samos. A foot precisely. It seemed to shake the whole place. Hedylus with his "Athens but not Athenian." Hedyle thought it rather good really, but the boy shouldn't know he had impressed her.

She said, "I mean my choice of Douris as permanent producer. Isn't he that really? He made a setting, gave us boards to tread on. You Hedylus, the fascinating and intellectual child of the Athenian—well, hetaira hardly suits it. Some call me an indifferent prostitute. Some a queen in hiding. There you have many mothers. Mothers. You have so many mothers that you shouldn't miss your father." Hedyle had rarely spoken of that predicament. She mentioned it now as blatantly as she had named Demetrius. "At least, darling, you may rest quiet in this. Demetrius simply isn't."

"I don't care who is or isn't, mother. It's your way about it."

"Way?"

"You don't seem to care—to have cared." But he couldn't say it. There was just one thing he couldn't say to Hedyle—"I've never had a father." Say, "my mother is a goddess," but it didn't salve it. He wasn't, in the world's eyes, anything.

Hedyle continued, "you're almost a prince here—practically the adopted son of Douris."

Douris. Adopted. Prince.

Hedylus said the words separately, then ran them all together, adoptedprincedouris. Words and then words. They slid and made strange running sound like water. Words were his preoccupation, his plague. Yes, mother was right. There was nothing for it. Life was lived in words, and lives multiplied in the word Athenian.

He said, "Athens must be pitiful in its downfall."

Athens. Athens. Athens. It was the sort of commonplace one made at Samos. To belittle Athens along with other famous inland cities gave them perverse satisfaction. Small, 'provincial' even, they were alive anyway. Their island was a kingdom. Douris as tyrant of Samos, an emperor. There was everything in Samos. Everything in one's own fervid mind, through which words went making water-music. The word Douris for example, recalled a stately arm, triangulated on the carved edge of a throne. Cushions at the back, and his mother sitting sideways. She couldn't ethically share the place, being—Hedyle the Athenian who wouldn't be labelled indifferent nor prostitute nor goddess.

"Mama, you seem a little upset."

"No. Nothing. I've been trying on various silvers. The metal is cold. To-night I seem to feel it. I'm getting too old for headbands."

"Mama!" The shock he put into his words was not feign-ed. "You wouldn't dare say a Cypris in a temple was old."

"Perhaps, darling, not old exactly. Only old-fashioned, somewhat."

"But mama, what's the matter?"

"I don't know. The blue bracelet doesn't go with silver. Or the silver doesn't go with the odd blue. Or the stones in this necklet are too heavy. I sometimes think women some day will parade in nothing. Not nothing. They're not beautiful enough now. In some ugly grey cloth. No colour. I can't believe in beauty." This last, even to him trained to ex-pect anything, was unexpected.

"Why mama, what's the matter?"

The room was blue, walls hung with blue, blue-finished woodwork and the painted doorway. The square of woven rug was from Assyria. The blue of the walls was reflected in the bare room-edges where the light caught. Hedyle was like some seated Thetis, under blue flowing water. The torch by the doorway went on and on, flaming up, falling a little. It reflected ripples of sparks in the bare edge of the marble, like phosphorescent trail of glowing fish in water. The boy was too white. Something in his mother had unnerved him.

"But, mama, we've been happy."

She said, "what's happiness?"

He said, praying she wouldn't catch some subtle overtone of insincerity, "happiness is just this, being near our Hedyle. Breathing the air she lives by."

Hedyle was too tired to turn and rend him. The boy was over-acting. Nevertheless, she managed "but, my darling, you look tired. When will you ever get over brooding on Alexandria?"

He was suddenly shocked. They had dropped that long since, their so authentic quarrel (it had lasted some months) over Alexandria. He was shocked at the crudeness with which his mother swung out this thing. It was so unlike her. She wasn't using the word Alexandria as a weapon. It was as if she had gathered anything, the first thing, some rough stone, illiterately, like a peasant terrified at some huge animal. It was as if she had seen in him suddenly, a wolf and illiterately was frightened.

"Mama! You treat me like a huge wolf—a terror seen in passing or worse still, the shadow of a terror whose outline isn't clear yet."

Hedyle drew her robe about her. The boy was uncanny sometimes. "I don't see terror in you. You are like light shining far at the end of a long tunnel. Everything was black until I had you." She had said this before, said it differently. But always with detachment, never speaking as a lover (which a mother should be) but as some wry philosopher.

Hedylus had had little opportunity of judging mothers. How did they, anyway, act on such occasion? A mother was an Aphrodite clothed in violet. A violet-veil should be cast across love that otherwise would blind one. Hedyle was too stark, too metallic in her beauty. She was some Athené who for wisdom's sake commits herself to childbirth. That was hardly what a mother should be. But could it matter? Life was lived in the turn of a syllable, in the vowelled run and beat and close of metres. Metres chased themselves across his brain like swallows in the sunlight, like swallows fleeing winter. So, too, they had escaped him . . .

"You've given me everything." This was always his answer to Hedyle when in any doubt of her ulterior motive. "You have, mother." What did she want, anyhow? She was staring at him.

"If you hadn't broken your head that day, you'd be another Sophocles." She had said that thing so often. She had constantly reminded him (as of some intellectual deficiency) of his radiant disobedience. Everything must date, it appeared, from primitive disobedience. He had tried fantastically to make up for that mark upon his forehead, branding him primitive, disobedient. How he had worked! For Douris technically but his searches through manuscripts, reading and compiling, his intellectual mainstay, was for his mother really. "Anyhow I am adequate, I have a trade like any honest goat-herd." He ran his finger across a gash whose appearance, affectedly forward-flung, untidy dark hair didn't really alter. The gash was there whatever he might do, might want to do about it. "If you hadn't broken your small head that day on the Acropolis, you'd be another Sophocles." Why Sophocles, anyway? He was tired of that particular application to his obvious defect. The gash was apparent at all times. It gave him a twisted, slightly cynical appearance. People *would* laugh about it. Sophocles! What indeed mightn't he have done if he had not been, psychically as well, so early blighted?

Talk of equality and democracy and the old Athens in its Periclean greatness! The rabble were always rabble. Try as you will, the rabble would spit on you and the rabble would roar and belch profanity. The gods even, had been belched at by the rabble. Leda before the birth-throes of Apollo. Apollo? Poor Hedyle. Maybe she didn't want me. She had glowered a moment since like any superstitious fish-wife who senses peril in a change of wind or a gull-plume fallen edgewise. Hedyle with clear mind and Athenian forbears had shied at a mere word. It was simply Alexandria.

"Mama," he said, speaking now as it were from nowhere, "I've given that up."

Alexandria. What was it but a word anyway? He would need equipment, money. Douris had trained him as highly efficient secretary. Hedylus had the keeping of many rare parchments, translations, compilations. He was helping Douris in his monumental history. It was something to save his face, his self-respect in Samos. "Almost a prince" was rot. He wasn't really. He was the son of an Athenian—"hetaira" wasn't the right word. You couldn't say Hedyle was an "indifferent prostitute." What was there left but "goddess"? Well, say he was the child of a goddess. That didn't bring anyone fame in these times.

He said again, "I've given up Alexandria."

She went on, not seeming to appreciate his sacrifice, "It's no use. Beauty perished. In Athens. You can't resurrect it."

He answered, perceiving weary argument, "you're quite right, mother."

The face. The face. The face. The boy's face was too white. Hedyle left him to draw away and scan it. Her garment made sheen and ripple like water over marble. Blue water flowing over pallid stone. Blue water over marble. She had sunk her keen intellect, her Athenian stonelike uncompromising nobility into flowing water. A woman with a mind must do. I couldn't give in to the fantasies of papa. What use is a woman if she isn't beautiful? Beauty now turned to regard itself as in a mirror. A painted figure with great eyes, wreathed in blue water-lilies. That assuredly was Hedyle. But Hedyle, too, was in that boy face. She saw in him, as in a polished mirror, herself certainly. I won't let him do it. He shan't get away.

"You really couldn't go to Alexandria."

"I said so, mother."

But something in the air had enervated Hedyle. As Lyda used to say, *The Furies walk on your grave.*

"I've not compromised."

"No one asked you to, mother."

"Nor should *you.*"

"I don't" (and prophetically a flame enfolded Hedylus) "intend to."

He wasn't going to compromise. He didn't know why he said it, what he had said. He seemed to feel himself shrink like smoke seen over water. Hedyle, his mother was blue flame and he was mere pallid smoke-stuff. I'm nothing. It seemed to himself that he was simply nothing. If I love Hedyle, I am something. When I don't, I am negated. She puts me out, as the sun a candle. She makes me a ghost at noon. He said, "Irene."

III

A WORD, A WORD, A WORD. A word spoken could change the interior of a room or the focus of a universe. This one (flung out) became luminous; he could almost touch it. It was round, not bevelled and shaped like Hedyle. Hedyle was his own name (it shone with jewel facets) with the exchange of one small letter. That letter made the difference. Hedylus—no—it was two letters really. I am Hedylus of Athens but not Hedylus the Athenian. Mother saw to it that Douris reared me a prince, nearly. What rot! Certainly, I am no prince in Samos. I saved my face by donkey-work, exploitation of old parchments which hold nothing so wonderful as the sea at nightfall. I wish to God, they weren't having that dreary banquet. Douris always overdoes things on these occasions. As if to prove we aren't provincial, aren't untutored, he will drag out the mouldiest of philosophies. That's where I help him. To-night, though . . .

"Irene," when he said it, made the room glower, become small and shrink beneath his fingers. I could tear mother's life to pieces like shredding a bit of frail cloth. What is she, anyway? I'll stay here (not go to Alexandria) as I've promised, for anyway I've this job with Douris. That shows I'm not essentially aristocrat. This holding down a job is my preoccupation. I'll stay here because it's my job, simply.

His mother said, "what are you pronouncing that name for?"

The room, the room, the room...this room and the other in the winter-pavilion by the quayside. Rooms held people and people held rooms. Names held people like rooms and Hedyle the Athenian exactly expressed his mother. Irene of Argos with a mother from Arcadia. Sikeledes. They all had—ancestors.

"Mama, I wish you'd tell me more of Clio, that aunt of mine."

"Why should I? Clio was indifferent. We played astutely; did what papa asked us."

Water-lilies should crown a name like Clio. It was the name of a Muse but somehow it became a little girl, her arms plunged into amber water, her hands pulling up dripping lilies. Clio should be crowned with water-lilies. The centre (or was it the edge?) of the name was smooth, cold in texture with the inapposite sheen of gold, the cores of water-lilies. Lilies had those cold smooth petals. "Clio" slid over your tongue like the texture of a white grape. "Irene" was shot with blue like a star shedding its darts of azure. "Hedyle"...he came back to Hedyle. Hedyle was asking him something. Just what was it?

"What are you pronouncing that name for? Irene."

He had said, "Irene." Whatever was the answer?

There was an answer to everything. So there must be an answer to this thing. He might say, "I said Irene, to see what you'd say." He might say, "I spoke the name, not thinking, as one may call on some obsolete deity in common talk, not meaning the lord of heaven when one says, 'O God.'" He might say, "I was experimenting with a new line and trying to get the feel and texture of the name, to find how it would go with iambic, monosyllabic, or archaic metre." He might say this, this, this. Each would be an answer. And none would be an answer. Mix them together, add and subtract. What *was* the answer anyway?

He said, "I was thinking of the child."

She said, "why that precisely?"

He said, "why what precisely?"

She said, "the child. In that tone of super-sophistication. Of almost patronage."

He said, "she is, to all intents and purposes."

She said, "she's a great over-grown, unnatural creature."

He said, "but, mother, she's so tiny."

She said, "over-grown, swollen with her frantic science."

He said, "science is a new Muse, one not to be treated lightly."

She answered, "Irene, the Muse of collecting dirty fishes, drying them on the quayside like any filthy urchin. Making a parody of manners and a practice of eccentricity."

He said, "her manners are perfection."

Hedyle made inevitable pronouncement, "perfection perished long since."

"O mother, let all that rest. We're young. We want expression."

Athens seemed a rope about his neck, strangling him. She couldn't have it both ways. It was "Hedylus, your manners, is there nothing of Athens in you," and then rending him with reminders of a lapse of some million of years ago. You can't hold it up against a child that it wanders after wild flowers. His mother wanted too much. Nevertheless, facing her in that lamplight, he knew (he always did, without premeditation) that she had conquered. There were no two ways about it. She just *had*. Why argue? Hedyle subdued him with no arrogance at this moment, but with a forward droop of small head that, he felt, somehow must be lifted on its brave stem. She seemed to have been baffled, beaten by alien elements. To him, over-sensitive to sound always, she had betrayed herself by unwontedly stressed syllable. The way a moment since, she had said "Demetrius." She didn't ask for pity, not even understanding. He must meet her half way. He said, "Irene is a strange girl."

She answered with metallic, ringing challenge, not seeming to give him credit for his gallant *volte-face*, "do you call her a *girl* in that outfit?"

He caught back his gallantly surrendered weapon and replied, as she seemed bent on quarrelling, "I see nothing irregular in the way she dresses."

She went on with it, as he knew she must do, "boys become more and more asexual. What is it that you're after? Have you no love of women?"

He answered automatically, "I haven't, frankly. Or I should say frankly, one woman has so surpassed them—"

"I don't want any of your studied rhetoric. I sometimes think you're like your great uncle, the Cyrenian. He used to hold forth in our garden. Under the winter-blossoms. It was desecration. There was a statue of Apollo used to go simply livid. Clio and I—she was named frankly for that odd Muse—used to note it. We were both silly children."

He urged again, "tell me about yourself and my aunt Clio."

"There isn't much now. She married that Paphlagonian (at least that's what I dubbed him) from the outer regions. He came, I believe, actually from Tarentum."

"In Greater Greece?"

"Near Sicily."

"I should like to have known—someone."

"Be thankful that you didn't. I was so crushed between the syllogisms of your bald-headed philosophic uncle and the arid pragmatism of your grandfather that I struck out for freedom. I want you to do as I did, maintain your own position."

"My own—" He hesitated. Bitterness, a knife, thrust at him. He sometimes thought his mother over-pretentious in her affectation, this studied negligence about the things that mattered.

"Position. You are frankly much nearer advancement, intellectual, material, as the foster-son of Douris—"

"Don't use that word, mama."

"What word, duckling?"

"I'm not theoretically a duckling and I'm, at your own confession, any man's son."

Hedylus felt the slight stiffening of muscles that he self-consciously noted when he knew his smile a forced one. Anyhow, this smile protected him. Hedyle couldn't hurt him. Nevertheless, he'd best drag back Irene.

"Anyhow, mama, do you suppose that girl would marry me?"

"*Marry?* When did you hatch your eggshell?"

"I'm not a mere sick child. You've treated me like one. I'm grown up."

Hedyle let a ripple from somewhere (was it laughter?) rise beneath the necklet with the studded dangling bead-ends of irregular chrysolite. She felt the stones like icy little knuckles on her bare flesh. Something had evidently happened. But what was it? It seemed to her this evening with the inspection of the steel-blue bracelet, that she had prophetic vision—she sometimes did have—of something that she couldn't name, that had no name, that eluded her mind as waves the smooth rocks. Her mind seemed smooth, polished. It had always been that. But thoughts tonight flowed over its hard surface. Had she been wrong, then? Had none of it, for all her brave show, quite worked? Had 'life' never even touched her? Did she remain, was she bound to always, just the daughter of a mouldy peripatetic Athenian? With no mother.

"What could mama ever have been like?" She asked the question suddenly, irrelevantly.

Her son said, "like you, Athenian."

"What is Athenian?" Hedyle in a moment forgot the banquet. It couldn't matter. Douris never mattered. He was courteous; in all particulars, a kingly person. He bored her, frankly. He had said and consistently maintained that to love Hedyle (for all her sophistication) was to love some wild bird. She had perched on his hand for a moment, being hungry. The next, she had eluded him, making wide curves toward heaven. He caught her one small nestling, trained and educated Hedylus like a young prince. She came back. She whirled in and about the court, the circle of scholars, merchants, intellectuals, soldiers, princelings that flowed back and forth, from and to Asia and to and from Europe equally. Her comings were erratic. One could always time her goings. She went when she was bored, simply. She had no authentic 'position', but there was nothing, no one, who held precedence over Hedyle. Some said she was an "indifferent prostitute," some said a "queen in hiding," some said a "goddess." She held all of these attributes lightly, passed swiftly from one to another. Nothing held her. One thing, simply. It stared at her in the blue room while Douris, tyrant of Samos, kept his guests waiting for their dinner. Its face was the face that a moment since had looked at her from polished silver. It was a painted column (washed clear of its bright blue, its rare vermilion) bathed in sunlight. It was the face of Hedylus.

"Athenian?" He repeated her question with rhetorical inflection. Then answered it, "O, that's what we would and can't be."

"I have it now. It's *you* that's made me shiver. It's not me that's getting old. It's you. You're trying to escape me."

"*Escape* you, mama?"

"Yes, I've felt it now for some time growing. *Is* it that girl, Irene?"

IV

IT MIGHT AS WELL BE IRENE AS ANOTHER; so he said, "it may be."

If it weren't (he had long since discovered) one thing, it was sure to be another. Hedyle had flown (ever since he could remember) into tantrums over nothing, a sandal-strap, a cloak-clasp, some slight irregularity of his garments, the fold of a peplum, the hanging of an outdoor winter-chiton. He was used to tantrums. He waited, breathing softly, "if it weren't one thing, then it would be another."

His friends—Sikeledes, for instance, rare fellow with the finger of a god scarring visibly his forehead. If he named Sikeledes, his mother would prod deeper than mere surface anger, drag out some more precious treasure, discuss iambics with callousness and cleverness. Iambics were not to be dealt with callously, Hedylus (even as a small thing) had discovered. Yet no subtly planned iambics could ever express the fervour of his vision. Technically, he felt he was not meant for greatness. Sikeledes, Posidippus even, both of his friends had a balance that he lacked. He cared too much for writing. Words followed him, filled the pallid substance of his skull with fervour. Sometimes he had to shake his dark short curls in running water to wash the words out.

"There is that special white stream on the mountain," his

29

thought sustained him, "that always will do." Again and again he had left the town, the wharves, markets set with outgrown, effete, or over-sensuous deities, to find his own God. This very morning he had washed names, inflections, colours of words out of his burning forehead. He didn't want to get into any fever with his mother. Her very name (his very name) upset him.

"Hedylus," he found himself pronouncing.

His mother snapped back, "Hedylus, what is the matter with you?"

He realized that his forehead, in a moment, would start flaming. Then there would be no use. If only his mother would discuss his two friends with him, be one of them, a Muse, a goddess to revive and encourage beauty. She would not have it. "Sikeledes is a pompous little gander, full of the new rhetoric of the Alexandrians. Posidippus has no breeding." She had dismissed them in a sentence. They were both, he had no least doubt in admitting, his superiors. He adored them. If only his mother could countenance these poets. There wouldn't then, be this odd severance in his forehead.

PART OF HIM WAS SUSTAINED BY HEDYLE. He was sustained, kept alive, revolving in her beauty. Part of him lived elsewhere. He was assured that if his mother countenanced his friends the breach would be better. It must heal sometime. I can't any more endure. The cold rivulet seemed washing his flaming forehead and spray blinded too-avid seeing. He would one day forget, drop down, be lost in some deep pool, some seething torrent, washed finally, torn and broken by the boulders, seaward . . .

"There were anemones on the upper slopes. I tried to bring them to you. But I was caught in the corridor by Douris with this long explanation and hastened to you. I didn't quite forget them."

His mother took a step toward Hedylus. "Why are you so enchanting?"

"If there is any reason for that, mother, you have only to regard your own bright mirror."

Again they were uncanny in their likeness, a live blue star reflected in a chill pool, a flaming red-lotus that sees its face pale and removed in a marble-oblong of fresh water. "I don't believe yet any man begot you. There's no man in you."

He said, "you wouldn't say that if you saw me wrestling. Why don't you ever come and acclaim our efforts?"

She said, "I've told you, all too often. The boorishness of these half-Asiatics bores me."

He said, "but there is beauty even if it isn't your sort. Why will you so abuse us?"

She said, "beauty quite perished one dark night in Athens."

He said, "don't, mama, dwell on that—the plague sweeping away your father and Clio, fleeing to Tarentum."

WHEN LYDA FINALLY DID ENTER, she was a bit breathless and said she had been three times up the terrace-steps looking for her mistress. "The moon is so odd. I was sure I had seen you,

wondered at your leaving without wraps, pursued and found
that ape-faced Sydonian servant (waiting-woman to Master
Posidippus' mother) leering at me. There were odd shadows
at the stair-top. Then the sea seemed like a plate of silver. I
wish sometimes there were our simple home-woods, the pine
and larch and the great oak-tree, about Sunium. This place is
too small and considers itself too civilized." Lyda had attained a manner from her mistress. She was quite happy in this
Samos. "I never knew such a dowdy line of waiting-women.
Not one with half a manner . . ."

"MANNER." What was life but that? The word, as pronounced by Lyda, sustained Hedylus, but half way up the hill-
steps, he drew back. He felt he needed support of some kind,
had wanted it from Hedyle, not having found it, had been
forced straight to Irene. After all, the girl has detachment,
sees me as an entity. Which his mother didn't. Mother is so
sharp. She is the moon at crescent. No one can deny that
beauty (as described by all the classics) must have mattered.
Helen, if she looked like that, had only to smile wanly.
Mother does look like Helen. I know it's all right. I know it
couldn't matter. Nevertheless his odd smothered inhibitions
made him draw back from Irene. It's so difficult, too, to tell
her. Not that such things *can* matter. She seems so old-
fashioned, never any inkling of worldliness, is some sort of
Hippolyta ungrown. She never will grow. She's quite as old
as I am and quite tiny.

He went on thinking of Irene. He held the name midway
in his thought between "Hedyle" and the word "manners" as

Lyda had pronounced it. What then was life but manners? Hedyle had so instilled a sort of technical attitude toward breeding in him that he was always baffled. Before this other . . .

Frankly it would have been better if there had been some one with whom to talk. One couldn't talk to Douris. One couldn't say to strangers, "my mother is a goddess, she had me with a god. I am nameless, bearing her name." Of course as her child with no—no father, I really had no right to full Athenian favour. She never says that. But I know. It's all very well, talking and arguing the matter, saying *"we* Hedylus, as Athenians." She is an Athenian woman. But what now is Athens? But, putting aside the disintegration of Athens, what am I as love-child of an Athenian? I suppose poor mother sustains this show to shield me. His thought went round and round. The whole thing brought him nowhere. And then the girl Irene.

I don't want to *marry* her but I wish she knew about it. How can one put the whole thing in a sentence? One can't say, "my mother—" well, what *can* one say? Everyone here knows all about us. It isn't that. It isn't that everyone knows. It's something else—he fumbled for expression. His very thought usually sustained him. Thinking self-consciously was an art, a subtle projection really, almost visible, of one's being. Thoughts eventually found expression in one's actions. Thinking, intense visual perception, was a kind of hidden histrionic talent. One thought and projected oneself outward in mere thinking. He might be walking ahead there on the stone step, where his thought preceded him. Here, he was bathed in moonlight. There, a bright torch, as a servant held it, would be casting sparks across a festive garment. The phantom preceding him might be some prince (Hedyle was right) returning from hunting, like Hippolytus, fresh and glowing from the mountains. I might be Hippolytus. He recalled the Attic drama and made almost involuntary gesture toward some waiting amphitheatre. But acting isn't my job. He went on slowly. He wanted to feel alone on this wide stairway.

We go on and on and on. But it seems lately I've stopped. I know mama's right in all her definitions. Beauty. And Beauty perished with the Athenians. I am a bastard. I am a bastard in the court of Douris. I am a bastard in the court of beauty. I know I can write more heavenly metres than Posidippus. Then why contend against him. Sikeledes is marked for certain greatness. There is the scar of the song-god written visibly on his forehead. If I serve Sikeledes, I serve the god of music. More than if I myself flame outward, break into the exact song that my brain prompts. I know that I can re-gather flowers from the mountains. It is necessary that the Muse's garland be rewoven. The heavy set lilies and the formal roses of Attic greatness have lost quality. They hang heavy on some dead Muse. We had better forget them, let them (for a time at least) rest in obscurity. There are exquisite blossoms, unnoted by the Muses. Take cyclamen. It has a sort of ember in its heart. Its name scars and scalds my forehead, like a red-star at daybreak. Other words have other manners with them. Goats and thyme-heads should enter into music. We have been too long enslaved to Athens . . . there, he perceived rebellion.

"I must frankly get this thing into some form of self-expression, just have it out with mother."

V

H E MET HIS MOTHER at the stair-top.
"You loitered."
"I was thinking."
"Thinking. Poems by moon-light?"
"Something of some such matter."
"Were you scanning the great lines of Euripides?"
"You guessed right."
"Which ones? And to what purpose?"
"The metres of the huntsman Hippolytus hanging offer-
ings to his goddess."

It was click-click with them. Stone-throw of query, inevitable ripple of response. Hedyle had to say "Athenian"
and Hedylus had to say this or this or this. Euripides, Hippolytus. Worn metres that held silver as the moon her ra-
diance. The choruses were crescent-shaped, horn-tipped,
tenuous and inevitable as the shafts of that same Artemis.
Say "Euripides and offerings to his goddess" and then
discover some little suavity, some gesture, standing aside in
some ultra-pretty fashion to show (without obviously saying
it) Hedyle that she was (it was too apparent to be mentioned)
a queen, a goddess rather. The huntsman twining flowers,
wood-lilies maybe, to his protective deity.

"Mother." Hedylus paused at the stone-basin that held the

Syrian jewel-fish. The fish swerved and twined and made intricate network; their fins glinting in the half-light repeated flash and shimmer of the iridescent blue cloth of his mother's new importation. "You never used to wear these things."

"What things?"

"So many amulets. This one." His thin fingers closed about her bird-wrist. He felt the unfamiliar smooth bevelled bracelet, "this odd one."

"I put it on, out of some curious fancy."

"Ah!" He had known there was something wrong here, mother cringing in the same sort of mental darkness, gasping like an illiterate peasant at some half-formed shadow of disaster.

"Mama! Why this one?" He held his mother's wrist, lifted it in the torch-light as one lifts a flower-branch toward divinity. He lifted his mother's wrist impersonally as one might raise the laurel to some temple statue. "Divinity." He thought that, said it.

"Why do you say, divinity?"

"I don't know. I do know. The bracelet rightly suits you. But take off all the others."

"Hedylus."

"Mama. I do know. You've been overdoing something. Lyda, take these bracelets." Hedylus gently pulled the heavy armlets from the right wrist. But she insisted on the others.

"I'll keep these on. I'll not go naked to assemblies."

He was re-arranging circlets on the left arm when Irene met them with "you look like Endymion and the half-moon. One side so iridescent in the torch-light, the other half in shadow."

Irene was perfection. He was right about her. There was no time for his mother to turn with half-sarcastic gesture, rend Irene with "you are the nymph Calliope" or some such hidden matter, knowing (as they all knew) Calliope was turned finally for some impertinence, into a wild bear. Mother

would slide insult into the most casual myth. She was sustained and clever. No one ever failed to see beneath the surface of
his mother's careful ironic speech. Hedylus must separate
them.

"Mama. You see, I said the right thing of Irene." They
were both staring at him.

"Which right thing—among so many?" Mama had
begun. Now she would be caustic. He must get her off this.

"I mean the perfection, simply, of her." He dared his
mother to turn and rend Irene. She stood flawless. Hedyle
surprised her son (it was odd she *could* surprise him) by turning with suave candour toward Irene, "your gown is exquisite."

Irene's dress was, so there was, for the moment, a truce
and for that reason as his mother swept away, Hedylus turned a little less avidly toward the slight girl. He saw her
remote, intricate, like the fish in water. She was remote, seen
under layers of perfection. She was Irene.

He saw Irene, appraised the little straight gown that fell
in metallic, inevitable ripples to the floor. The dress was (and
Hedyle knew it) perfect. Irene wore no jewels. Her head was
wound with a simple band of gold-cloth. She was too simple,
in a way too childlike. Hedylus took a deep breath. "Irene."
She was a star obliterating night with incandescent glamour.
But only a star. Hedyle was the goddess, half in shadow,
glowing and diminishing. She lit the whole sky. Irene was
perfect in her small way. Blue-star darting its azure but with
limitations. He saw Irene as metres sensed at night-time, incandescent, pulsing and intransient. Never quite caught. He
saw her veiled as with her own perfection.

"Mother is so odd. She never, never means it." Why
must he protect his mother, say that starkly?

"I know, I do know," she met him half-way. "All
mothers are that."

Irene was fashionable in the lamplight. She would

change, become the wild bear at a moment's notice. No doubt she was already planning tomorrow's escapade.

"Are you spearing eels or wrasse-fishing in the morning?"

"Eels, I imagine. I thought tonight, as it was all so brilliant, I might even fish before dawn."

"In those things?"

She said, "you know I never wear things like this save under strong compulsion."

He said, "I'm sick of all this."

She said, "they're half a dozen (with Demetrius) going to have dinner in the long pavilion."

He said, "Demetrius?"

She said, "the delegate. From Athens. He wants a sort of critical assembly to judge all your poetry."

"Whose poetry?"

"Yours, Posidippus, Sikeledes."

This was the last straw, really. "I can't come."

"But Demetrius is funny."

"Ah!" This was too much. He couldn't see fun in this thing. Demetrius. His mother had pronounced the name, earlier in the evening as in despair that she couldn't possibly pack into those four small syllables all the scorn that the sheer combinations of sound (apart from the thing they signified) stirred in her. Demetrius. There was tragedy, mystery, epos, in the way she said it. Irene had changed that. Hedyle, it seemed now, had gone in with set face and over-emphasized dignity, inconsequently to meet something that was—funny. Irene marred the epos.

"Do you know him?"

"We talked in the outer atrium before Douris came with the rest of the legation. He really does amuse me. He calls me a sea-anemone, inshelled like a sea-urchin. He says, I wear the garments of a sea-urchin to conceal divinity." Sea-urchin.

She was that. Mother was right. Calliope, little shaggy wild bear sleeked down for the occasion. This was Irene. Hedylus was right when he maintained Irene was perfection. His mother also was right in her pronouncement, "she makes a parody of manners." Her manner to his mother had been perfect. But she was making, it was obvious, a parody of something. Was it of Hedyle?

His mind flashed back and back. Athens. Irene wasn't—put it in a nutshell—Athens. Athens remained (in his vision) sharp in outline, a jagged yet defined picture, such as one might remember, sighting life for the last time, through some catastrophe-stricken wall. Hedylus seemed to see Athens as through a wall that's broken. I suppose that is due to the fall and the sudden jerk it left in me, jerk out of babyhood perhaps into real consciousness. Lyda hadn't altogether been responsible. He had strayed for wild-flowers, against her strict injunction. Soldiers didn't, he had been rigidly disciplined, disobey their masters. Still, even then, he hadn't accepted finally this idea of military rightness. Why shouldn't soldiers, seeing wild-flowers, go and get them? His hands had been filled with winter-poppies, those crimson embers that scar the Acropolis (burnt-out fire of some destructive conquest), scar of her own death-wounds. He was regarding one that fluttered single petals in a little fresh wind, a red-butterfly, when the shale failed him. His small trim sandals had trod (wild-goat-like) a little too unguardedly toward the already crumbling wall of the Brauronia.

When Lyda found him, the poppies and his wound made one sacrificial colour against a splintered pilaster. The marble left its mark on the boy's forehead. It was still there. The early witticism (so tediously repeated) made psychic-wound within him, "child, if you hadn't broken your head, you'd be another Sophocles."

He thought again, why Sophocles exactly? Broken

forehead. Why not someone else, Theodorus, Pericles even? Again he ran an incredibly slender index finger along his forehead. I'm in bits, it's useless. He went back always in his thought to that one moment. Athens remained fixed in memory, a picture seen through a fallen doorway. The house falls in a volcano, shaking, riven perhaps, and one vision stays fixed. Perhaps of sun-steeped vineyards, climbing to a hill-top or of the hill-crest itself in its silver of white snow, or of some unwonted trivial incident, a dog limping, screaming perhaps at its own ripped flank, or some chance beggar taking occasion to rob an honest merchant's toppling fruit-stall. Something stays fixed in consciousness with any severe early misadventure. With him, it was this simply: at five, I woke out of a pleasant half-world into reality. The Acropolis had marred him. He thought always, it was that one broken column that had dealt the death-wound.

"For I've never been alive," he said to himself frankly. "I've always wandered in a half-state, never faced reality." But reality here faced him. He was contradicted even at the moment of phrasing the thought. It was the girl Irene.

She said again, "the place is crowded. It is too hot indoors. Posidippus bribed some of the kitchen-servants (you know his way) to send in dishes to the long pavilion. Won't you have dinner with us?"

He said, as if she hadn't just this minute told him, "who's us?"

She said, "Sikeledes and the others. All we can rescue from this conference. Won't you come with us?"

Hedylus remembered his mother, her face set in hatred toward Irene, and Irene's half-jibe; moreover he recalled as well, Hedyle's even more bitter antagonism to those "others." He wanted so awfully to break with the whole matter. But he hadn't the heart to. Not just this night. Tomorrow. Later. Why didn't they go off and leave him to it? He must stick for the moment anyway, to Hedyle. He wouldn't compromise. How she had said, "Demetrius." He had told his mother that he wouldn't compromise. Not tonight, anyway. Well, he would tell Irene.

"You're all very well without me."

"Maybe. But you. Are you, Hedylus, well without us?"

He hadn't thought of it in that light. Hadn't dared to think of anything as being necessary. But his mother. His mother hated Irene—and there was that ape, Demetrius.

It wasn't Irene that he turned against but his own determination not to let down Hedyle. Not tonight anyway. Let down. Who was he letting down? He was just nothing in this. Something had been devised, was already set in order. He had no part really in it.

"I think I can manage well enough for one night. I have some more work."

"You've done enough verse for that one screed for Douris."

"It isn't that work." How tell her what the work was? He only just this moment saw his real work. "I have work." And he left her rather starkly.

VI

HAVING COMMITTED HIMSELF SO FAR, there was nothing for it but stoically to continue. He didn't think anyhow, he wanted dinner. The idea of Demetrius bored him. He forgot that he had been out all afternoon, dripping with the hill-snows, had scarcely found a moment to change for dinner and had then been interrupted by Douris with the message for his mother. Then out again, down and down the hill-steps (his work-room was in the scribes' hall nearer Douris) and an unexpected half-scene with his mother. It wasn't, in the light of former incident, to be felt too acutely. After all, there were days and days . . . his mind, formulating thought, refused to formulate exact and careful picture. Something in him, clouded like the smoke from a volcano marring jonquil meadows, when he thought of Hedyle. After all, she is alone. Or after all, it wasn't her fault that she had me. Or after all, what if I am a bastard? Or after all, mother's beautiful and distinguished and a woman can't be everything.

Something clouded his precise feeling, something in him was self-blunted, a self-imposed veil covered his too-clear seeing when he thought of the Athenian. Hedyle remained, and would remain in thought, synonymous with Athens.

"After all, I might have done more for her."

He went down the side-shale. It was full moonlight,

though the moon casting amber glow, remained somewhere hidden. Like the "others" she had withdrawn from the crowd, the great massed company of giant stars about her, and was dining elsewhere. With what, he conjectured, secret lover; Endymion (Irene had just named him) seemed too wild, too wayward a lad for her sophisticated greeting. Hedylus felt (following the familiar crevices of the half-natural stairway) that this place was no medium for meetings other than astutely artificial. Everything seemed fixed, static in stage-set atmosphere. The stairs, the garden, the terraces were, he had always thought, like some amazing amphitheatre. The whole thing was a stage, tiers on tiers of terraces, amphitheatre seats above sunken pavements, the inevitable statues. Every corner of the island was exploited, all but the very rigid hill-peaks where constant melting snows made foot-hold too difficult for Douris' rather formal attempts at wildness. Once in so often they must climb the hill-path, make some sort of Dionysiac gesture; this getting back to nature. There was one other amazing wilderness only, on the island. Should he chance it?

His work? He had said to Irene that he had work. His poetry remained in his thought, along with his mother, unformulated, vague. Poetry? Hedylus didn't know why his attitude to Hedyle should have crept in. He supposed, facing it frankly, that his work was his secret mother, the mother that answered when he claimed her, that gave him return for caresses, that never grumbled at his belt-clasp. A Muse, was (wasn't she?) a sort of elder sister and Hedyle was more (wasn't she?) sister than mere mother? A Muse was a sister, a Muse was a lover, and a mother ought to be a sister and a lover. But she wasn't. No one ever had a mother like that. A sister would do perhaps, someone like Irene...his instep caught an unexpected bit of brushwood.

The early irises...this odd end of the garden always was

self-consciously neglected... has Irene been here?... were his disconnected thoughts. Then he jerked the brittle, pliant reed-stem from his sandal. Irene's the only person ever comes here, she takes the damned place seriously. After every sort of wild-flower. She says we have things that they haven't got in Argos. Their native pansies she says though, grow bigger and straight down to the water. She thinks she likes her mother's home, Arcadia, better.

His thoughts, his thoughts, his thoughts. His preoccupation with his own thoughts annoyed him. Why couldn't he just let go and love something? He didn't love Irene. He *saw* her perfectly, retained her by some magic in his mind, used her as a sort of visual magnet. He could draw things to him, thoughts, with the focus of Irene. The name was detached, a bowl set like that one at the stair-head to contain (instead of gold fish) moving particles of swift thought. With Hedyle, it was different. But that too was too complex, too involved an emotional state, to be exactly labelled "loving." Love and love and love. Poets wrote about it. Sikeledes. The Attic drama had fumbled toward exposition. The thing was too subtle really, for expression. Electra. Brother and sister. The love of some wild mistress like Medea. All that was dramatized. But love as he wanted it...he hadn't even superficially compassed the thing his soul had sought for. It seems that I've been looking for something, all these years. From the first moment of my first mistake. I went scrambling after wild-flowers. Poppies weren't what I wanted...what was it? I've been looking for it every day since that day. He made the turn by the second stairway. The sea made mirror-reflection of the moon, though the moon still remained half-hidden. He might, he conjured, just, just see to read them.

The usual twist and slide through the bushes. He could do it with his eyes shut, in smiting noon-light; so here, in this noon-moon of amber, he could so easily guide his sinuous young limbs along the length of old pavement that had led (still did to the initiate) down to the lower water. The stone-path had been neglected many years since, long before Hedylus and his mother came to Samos. Heavy box-trees had been formally planted, almost (it seemed) in some mythic age, and their great low sturdy roots had obscured the old paving from the stair-side. The upper stairs led straight up the hill to one of Douris' comparatively recent little playgrounds, a circle of rustic deities and vines that had grown sturdy in Hedylus' memory and more statues that made (the other side) a half-circle toward the mountains. The mountains themselves, owing to the devious roadways and the still somewhat old-fashioned ideas Douris cherished as to goatherds, remained inviolate. The hill above and the sea below (just in these inaccessible patches) were his birthright.

Some old and sophisticated deity cherished this neglected sea-shelf. It's funny no one ever coming to it. He still made that formal protest (he had always made it) as he slid across the pavement. The paving, owing to the heavy black bush above, was almost invisible; one sensed its formal pattern. The down-slope was dry, for all the fall of rain above and the icy rivulets on the hill-side. Hedylus noted each change of temperature, the notch where the old paving joined a patch still older, the slide that meant elbows very close and that final rather perilous smothering in the last, thickest part of the bush-tunnel; this as always, preceded tumbling into the open.

The open space was as always. It looked more dangerous than ever. The rock was a slippery slice of tilted amber in this moonlight, and the sea below him was a heavy plaque of silver. If he slid too suddenly forward he would fall, he was certain (for all his knowledge to the contrary), straight on to shining metal and be shattered outright. A bird falling from a nest might so, for one moment, contemplate its long predestined way of dying. "Everything's decided for everything beforehand."

He said that, staring hypnotized at shining water. Why try to wander or try to gain the thing I now have? I have the thing they look everywhere else for, right here on island Samos. Alexandria and the prattle of the new art, the very sound and at times illuminating statements of his friends, the beauty visibly branded on the forehead of Sikeledes became, at such tense visionary moments of fulfilment, so much withering tinsel. Reality remained. Would always. You might prate of goatherds in the latest Alexandrians or you might chant your Homer. Beauty wasn't, in the long run, much affected. That was why he had stated so decisively to Irene that he had some "more work." Work? He smiled as he thought how easy it was to dupe them. Those poems he had proffered as his best effort to Posidippus, were faked modernity. Perhaps they were reading them now (how funny) in the long pavilion. Hedylus closed his eyes lest his prevision of the fall on polished silver should unnerve him. I always took this last jump dubiously...

He landed again with firm-planted feet, with lithe heels (rigid slim twin arrows) pointed upward, with flexible sandal-toes planted firm on hard sand. His hands, as always, struck flat on the ground and as always, left firm imprint, carved symbol as of hands praying, as on some archaistic altar.

Hedylus closed his eyes but knew, once he lifted his forward-flung head and gazed about the irregular little sea-edge, that walls would rise to left, to right. He would be penned in to the left, to the right. The sea would never pen him in, would stretch its iridescent blue—no, it was now night. The sea would be sombre wine or silver dimmed into half-translucence, from this angle. The sea that was ordinarily lapis would be covered with streaks of purple...like, like...with his closed eyes and heart pounding (excitement of extravagant plunge) he asked what it was the sea recalled to him.

Hedyle's robe was it, that this evening had taken shades of purple? Iridescent (not her usual defined blue)—she had seemed like Thetis. Again his opened eyes challenged the silver water. "Tell me, what's it all been?" He asked that with teeth clenched, with body tense and (suddenly he realized) shivering. What's this that's happening to me? The sea looks like mother's mirror. I know I've been wet but that's so often happened. His hands still remained flat, making their imprint as of two palms praying; the knees kept their firm half-crouch; the head flung back remained solid like some marble runner. Then he broke from his frozen dream-state. "I have come on business."

He had been through scene on scene on this shelf; mostly of his own making, stages and rooms of his own peopling, halls and streets and street-corners filled with phantoms of his conjuring. Sometimes there were real people. He recalled, in particular, one occasion with Posidippus...not that the boy had meant it. How could he? He was my own friend.

"That was why I understood his saying it, understood what he meant." However, Hedylus then had not been so philosophical, had stumbled for words to answer that odd query, "Who *was* your father, anyway?" Hedyle was right. Even in those days, Posidippus showed regrettable lack of tact. You can't say, "I don't know." Posidippus jeering, "some god maybe" had given him the clue. Hedylus had answered simply, "maybe." There had been further ironical illusion and Hedylus, as might have been expected, landed finally inglorious on the hard sand. That was almost the first and last time the three had been here together. Hedylus affected a sort of distaste for "that dark hole." Sikeledes frankly hated the final forward jump down. The leanings of Posidippus were for open ground, wrestling, games with the townspeople. Hedylus kept this place his secret. It was linked irretrievably in his memory with his first Acropolean downfall, and this other. Hedyle? Hedyle. He said"Hedyle" over and over and, opening his eyes and rising to his lithe heels, repeated, "I must get the business over."

VII

THE "BUSINESS" WAS A SHEATH OF PARCHMENT which he deftly unearthed from a little hollow in the rock-side. The extravagant moonlight seemed to be exactly focused on the small sand-square. Hedylus stepped from the shadow like some actor (his usual method) toward applause and recognition. He stepped forward as if awaiting some howl of excessive welcome and he bowed ironically (as his way was) to the stark sea.

The sea lay stark and silver and he quelled an impulse simply to walk forward across its polished hard floor on to . . .something other. There must be some other world, some form of expression whose materialization would answer to its stark appearance. Here everything carried, as the crescent-moon its shadow, its own contradiction. Things weren't (it was obvious) what they so oddly seemed. The appearance must be perfectly justified, exactly materialized . . . somewhere. Yet he mustn't be tempted at the moment by the fascination of sheer philosophic quibbling. He'd come here for the poetry. Hedylus unwound the parchment. The sky's clear enough to read by. But I already know them. He proclaimed softly:

Helios,
king,
lord of the other-world's white ivory portal,
people of greater wit and will proclaim you
god,
anax
and immortal;
for me there's nothing left
but finite things,
the shimmer of a petal
or a feather
dropped from a floating bird-wing
or some little
shells
streaked dark sea-red and purple.

Helios,
who claims the world,
I,
I a mortal
have nothing for you
such as scribes indited
in magic books,
no line of priests
nor lighted
torch
nor the brazier;
I have myself;
the azure
heaven
has no, no heart to doubt you,
so I,
pity me,
see,

senseless and lost
without you.

I sing,
not as a priest of other-times
but this
scroll of small worth
contains you;
it holds you as the poppy
the bright dream,
the reed the river;
I have no other
offering,
no hecatomb of mighty steers;
I have myself;
yet all the seers
of Delphi
could not give
greater,
O father.

Luminous,
hear;
in other lands
wan limbs
and stricken
hailed you
and proclaimed you
master of healing,
Paeon;
as of yore,
see,
see
my hands uplifted

to implore
your bounty;
(yet could I dare
to face you,
smitten sore
with arrows
of your beauty?)

Lovely,
most dear,
my slight song has no end but its own singing,
my stricken heart no being
and my soul
no light
but from the aether
of your dwelling;
compassionate,
hear
this hail
and this farewell.

The lilt and fall of lines brought Hedylus face to face with himself again, with water glowing silver, with moonlight casting light (apparently from deft artificial arrangement of dark screens) from a sliced rock above him. Lit and fervid with the lilt of the tense irregular metres he looked (his usual method) outward for some visible sign of that invisible audience toward which again, receiving no sign of approbation, he bowed (as his way was) ironically. They're no good really. The thing's all in my head. It won't get out. My achievement is a candle flaunting itself in the bright sun-face of my vision. It's no use. He shivered. The things *are* bad. There's no use softening toward them. Let them go straight to god with all their fiery godhead with them. Their divinity

doesn't show on the stark parchment. Their bodies remain
shameless, the garments of metre and stanza leave them
naked. Well, god accepts the naked soul provided that it's
flaming. Poems go nowadays like that girl they brought to
Samos. Wrapped in grave-cloths. Mama kept the bracelet.
He fluttered the stiff parchment. A word flickered at him. It
recalled Hedyle. Blue lily. He read further.

Grown in a shadowed portal
where gods are,
lily,
mysterious flower,
are you more wondrous
than the mountain one,
the gracious moon folds up
and the bright sun
unfolds at dawn?

Though Hesperus rises
to proclaim you fair,
O wild, wild lily,
tell me, have you more
enchantment
than the holy precinct-flower
who keeps her fragrance
for the worshipper?

O wild, wild lily
and bright spirit-flower,
how can I hope to know
which is more rare,
the one who spills her fragrance on the air
for passing birds and stars and flowing water,
or that proud blossom

who must wilt to hear
the sorrows
that the passing people bear?

Blue lily
and wild lily,
tell me where
I can entreat a sage
who'll tell me whether
the blue flower
or the wild-flower
is more fair?

He had meant that for Irene and Hedyle, a contrast, but it was trifling. He hadn't got the thing he really wanted. The thing was a flower lost, without earth, body to grow from. It lacked too the fashionable sprinkling of deity, the names thrown in like so many gems set in the solid hammered metre of the poem-stuff. However he looked upon it, the lines had no place in poetry, only with pure thought whose very power lies in the fact of intangibility; water-drops, that change, are lost with the sun-shifting or pulsing with glow and iridescence like transient rainbow (as they now did) in his tired head.

Words made their special glow and iridescence; *that* warned him he was tired out with thinking.

Glow and iridescence. He couldn't think any more. He closed his eyes. The whole thing's manifestly futile. The metres are chopped, irregular. I must burn them. Rocks could be set into oven-shape; he had the old steel and flint left from boyhood. Games here, building fires and wrecking ships and calling the dead of Athens to arise and hail him—not Hedylus—some other...some Periclean child of mighty forebears...my father was...my father is...he had been obsessed with the name, the secret was a sort of talisman to the infinite. If I had a father—if I had had a father—flames should rise and cleanse his soul of its last infantile obsession, its childish fantasy.

My verse; this is not good. The idea, the thing I worship is so near that the verse makes a veil across it. I won't proffer these things to Sikeledes. They're too good, not good enough; I can't have them fighting like vultures over fresh bones. Yet they're right. Metres must be dealt with honestly. I have used mine as a sort of invocation. It's tampering with divinity. I can't be a poet and a magician. I'll be one or the other. Not both. I'll sacrifice, in sacrificing them, my very soul, the pulse and dart and element of divinity. I'll be strict and staid after this. He re-arranged the parchment.

The stones were easy to place edgewise. The fire was an old miracle. He crumpled the pages and found wood, a stick of old myrtle and some sprays that had died among the living bushes. The early buds mingled with last year's berries, still fresh and livid, pearls untouched here by wild birds. The place was remote, inaccessible, even the birds decried it. There were bigger berries, huge bushes, the wild birds knew, in the hedge of box above stairs. Above his head the impenetrable thicket of old boxwood held many wild things, small furry mammals, moles and exquisite mottled rabbits. (Mama once had a coat patched from tiny mole-pelts. It seemed extravagant but lovely over her soft stuffs.) There were lizards. Little serpents. The place was alive with hidden secrets, his own divine cavern. Here I am alone, have been always, after the others grew up. I never have done. I am always renewed in this fragrant covert. It's mine simply. He had never worshipped so singly, been so simple-minded. I love the things so much, they so really do express me that I'll burn them. He was wandering about meanwhile, fitting in rocks, piling brush-wood, examining the parchment.

No, this won't do. "Irene" darted at him. It was like

burning live blue hyacinths. These other pages to Irene are and aren't quite right. Anyhow, they aren't sanctified to burning. They're not, somehow, purified. There might be more to them. I might keep them, work on them, perfect them, and then burn them if I want to. He shuffled the parchments, tore here a bit, there. He piled certain pages back into the original crevice. "Irene shall be safe there." He closed the little crevice with the rock and piled myrtle-branch across it. No one could get the parchment. He found fresh weed and hid the crevices.

"*Fair by the rock-shrine* was very good. I'll let it rest." He murmured, meanwhile, remembered bits of the discarded parchment, "*holy on Delphic ridges, heart and lover.*" Words pulsed at him, dart and fervour, *laurel-bud*, the irregular edge of a broken line that struck at him like forked lightning. The things held his own heart-beat, his own blood and fire. He mustn't any more regard the pages or he would regret his peculiar decision. *Ember of rock-flower.* Let it go now. Solemnly he re-arranged the flat stones and, after deft preliminary with flint and dead grass, burnt the pages.

BLUE SMOKE PULSED UPWARD. Hedylus stood, a young priest, invoking daemons, propitiating dead souls. I think Hedyle's dead really. Her eyes are blue like water on a lotus. I don't see how such beauty can contain anything but immortality. She isn't in that sense living. When she said "Demetrius," I saw she was dead, had died in Athens. "Demetrius," when she said it, brought a veil of terror and then a stark frigid unreality. Something hurt her. She died, I am sure, in Athens. She has never loved the Tyrant. What is Douris? He is no more to her than the very chair she sits in, is as much certainly. For all her unearthliness, she clings to reality, to material things. It seems a contradiction. Irene on the other hand, has glacial eyes, eyes that don't pity. She can't pity for she has never been born. Irene hasn't been born yet, Hedyle is dead already. It's the one or the other. I'll stick to the dead for I am dead already. Athens is dead already. I'll stick to Athens and I'll stick to Hedyle.

HE STOOD, leaned heavily wounded, his shoulder pressed against the roof-rim that was the uplift of his own familiar cliff-edge. His shoulder sunk, supporting, bruising him, as against the heavy edge of some gigantic altar. His head wearied, flung (that sharp wound) forward. Everything centered curiously in the forehead. Lovers, notably Sikeledes, had spoken of heart's fervour. They felt evidently elsewhere. Lovers spoke now openly of heart-beats. With him, manifestly, it was different. Emotion rose from the heart perhaps but it ended always in the head, blinded, drove one to this inner vehicle. This thing inside was like a crystal-stone shut in an ivory box. His inner self was safely lodged in one stone. It was iridescent, a little like Irene's sea-shells. It was heartless like Irene.

With that stone (his eyes were closed, his head still pressed against the cliff-edge) it almost seemed that he could see past and present equally as in one continuous eye. What could it matter if one were dead or living? Continuous intermingling circles, like those seen on some fine-spun web.

Circles of clear spinning with the sun aslant them, making threads of silver. The web to catch his thought was just of such a spinning. Pallas was goddess of woven work, of tapestry. She was this defined thing as well, the crystal, her own grey eyes precisely. She *saw* with those grey eyes. Grey eyes nearer Hedyle's in colour than Irene's. . . .

His head, his head, his head. Why couldn't he love—someone? Posidippus with his worship of odd loves, Sikeledes with his various lovers, Douris loving Hedyle, Hedyle loving. . . who, what but Athens had ever really trapped Hedyle's affection? Hedyle. Why had she stumbled like that, this evening? Just before the banquet. Was it that name, Demetrius? I haven't had my dinner. Is that the reason for this creeping nausea? I sometimes think the simple way out would be to slide down simply, not look for the last irregular bit of rock-edge, roll off. Fall like a spilt birdling. Fall from the nest of human intercourse, human thought and thinking, and be shattered simply.

VIII

HIS THOUGHT WENT ON and on and on. Like the blue smoke-trail, it went blindly upward. He stood here below them all, on a lower step (as it were), facing divinity. His step downward, he knew, by odd contradiction, foreshadowed a step upward. Hedyle was right. Better have some interesting fable in the background, some half-myth, some half-authenticated father than to know simply it was someone even like this Douris. Douris was in all particulars an excellent example of what a parent should be. How utterly boring and febrile if his father had been Douris. Well, Douris wasn't, for, after all, they had come across Douris some time in his fifth year. Demetrius? Mother seemed somewhat intent on proving that he wasn't. Was it just because he might be? The name still followed Hedylus but what was the little man (Irene was right) but funny? His nose was indigo. Straight odd hips, suave under his elegantly wound garment, sandals with too ornamental trapping, rings and the unusual armlets. Demetrius' face was that of some little withered Dionysus, somewhat wistful and withal not without charm. His eyes were fox-like, sly, authentic eyes of some over-burdened intellectual. Demetrius, it was evident, had thought clearly. His eyes long ago, when Hedyle was in Athens, might have inflamed her curiosity. Little boring eyelets that went down and down and all the time the rest of the man was a pitiful mass of contradictory elegance. Elegance, power, the strange odd leer and the still exquisite line of somewhat fragile shoulders. A funny little ambassador of greatness. For Demetrius was, Hedyle couldn't absolutely disprove it, in his odd way, adventurous.

Hedyle was always trying to disprove something. What was it she was after? Well anyhow, he'd just caught that exact glimpse of Demetrius, though he hadn't told his mother. Nor that other thing, that odd exact formal invitation to them all, the three of them, to go to Alexandria. Demetrius needed secretaries, various skilled rhetoricians, students versed in philosophy. He could have the pick of Athens but he wanted something different. "A little less wary, a little less weary," as Demetrius himself so aptly phrased it. Posidippus had reported the whole conversation and he himself (at the boat's landing) had had that authentic glimpse of the odd creature. Not that he'd tell Irene—nor his mother.

Blue smoke pulsed upward. Well, that was the utter end of Alexandria. Hedyle needed him. He would stick to Hedyle, fight and lunge and bitter antagonism to the contrary. I know it's impossible to defy her. Maybe I *am* a coward. I'll stay here. I'm not strong enough to fight her. Hedyle has hinted everything, told me, in spite of her affected candour, nothing. Athens and Athens and father was fantastic and Clio laughed at our Cyrenian uncle and we both adored the statue of Apollo and Lyda taught us that we mustn't ever try things; little wild berries for example, gleaming jewel-like, iridescent on strange bushes that mustn't, under any circumstances, even so much as be looked at. *She* had never (she had often hammered at his child intelligence) disobeyed anybody, wandering after wild-flowers. And so on. And so on. Hedyle was exasperating with her insistencies, with her affectations. But he must stick to her.

He felt oppression slightly lifting at this final definite decision. It was a heavy stone, he recalled blithely; the poems would not, could not escape, like this blue smoke, from beneath its downright pressure. The poems to Irene were safely housed, safely tombed within the temple-shelter of that cave-depth. He would place more seaweed carefully across the stone-head. So that should he, even tonight, slip down on his perilous upward crawl, to some heavy sea against which he would fall (be by its heavy lapis surface shattered), those poems would be forever unredeemed. The three of them informally borrowed and more formally had a way of declaiming the metres of each other. Irene might (his thought lightened) even now think (should the worst happen) Sikeledes had wrought them.

No one would know him nor remember him for any but his most ribald metres. He had for common occasion a separate parchment, open to all eyes; "Limb-relaxing gout" was a particularly favoured piece when Douris was in gay mood. His "Life is but vain, unless I drink and drink again" would fitly represent him to his generation. Hedyle would guard that manuscript. If, clambering up the ill-defined and slippery cliff-edge, something should assail him, dizziness, some vertigo, some old blindness (reminiscent of that plunge forward from the Acropolis) and he should slide to be shattered on the heavy sea-surface that would not, he was sure, break open to receive him; if he should fall, himself broken, to the surface of that lapis sea, none certainly would be the wiser for it.

Opening his tired eyes, he saw the apparition.

IX

OLD TRAINING SO FAR SUSTAINED HIM that he spoke blithely. "It is curious to find one of Demetrius' company on this coastside."

Opening his tired eyes, Hedylus had seen simply, a heavy figure outlined against a silver floor, a plaque across which he had some moments since decided it must not be difficult to walk, that must lead (after the decision that poetry was worthless) to some other realm of thinking. The figure, standing with arm triangulated under a heavy cloak, was so simply part and parcel of the thing the sea appeared—plaque-like silver that intelligence informed him was only fluid substance...that, arguing in trained efficient manner, it seemed logical that as the sea wasn't what it appeared (such solid silver) so this, so solid and apparently conventional appearance, must hide some other quality.

The sea must be treated, nevertheless, conventionally as water; one would, for all one's exact fantasy of visualization, take a boat for example to carry one across it. So this, appearance to the contrary, was some delegate, some half-civilian soldier (from his bearing), one of the usual formal legates, ambassador, most likely, of Demetrius' delegation. Old training sustained Hedylus and old habit. One would inevitably take a boat to cross water even although one knew (in some other heaven) that water was no more like the substance of one's earthly knowledge than rain from chrysolite. Materialized, this god to whom lately he had been chanting verse, must be treated like a mortal.

"Demetrius' company apparently has bored you." He could go on with it, this way anyhow, blithely. How did the creature get here, anyway? If he were (as supposition must later positively prove) one of the delegation, he must have got a boat, a boatman. Which one?

"Was it old Karo brought you round the cliff-edge?" Karo was the only fisherman who ever penetrated this rocky edge, who found any profit in its barren seclusion. It was partly because of some eccentric idea he had of ferrets. He observed them from the water-edge and had lately exposed the corner, just one after this one, to Irene.

"Karo, as I recall, has the most trying habit of forestalling strangers. We have often warned him not to blight the island welcome (as Douris would extend it) by dragging poor unsuspecting foreigners round our cliff-edge. Douris likes having parties. A sort of formal informalization. You know what I mean. Believing or pretending to believe that the old gods matter." The apparition must be treated with respect. It was such a lordly vision. After all, he had perhaps manifested himself here for some odd reason. What then, exactly, was it?

"Why, if you will condone my crudeness, have you chosen this barren cliff, this edge of water? Our master, Douris, has so many exquisite seclusions, paths and water-steps laid out below the gardens. How, if I may so crudely ask it, did you get here?"

The heavy head bent forward on the column of strong throat, recalled no actual fashion of the moment. This god had chosen shape from former greatness; Athens in decadence, Corinth at its moment of high flowering had no such exact and powerful image to redeem its over-intellectualized sheer prettiness. There was nothing (could conceivably be nothing) of affectation, of intellectualized fragility, in this solid and commanding presence. The phantom chose his shell most wisely. God, appearing naked in white elegance, wouldn't have surprised Hedylus. God appearing cloaked as an ambassador of Douris, quite unnerved him. "I mean, I'm sorry that I missed you in the throne-room."

The words, the words, the words. Hedylus listened to his own words, his nicely spaced dialogue, his pauses that had been just long enough to allow of answers and that had been swiftly sustained, prolonged, woven into monologue, when no answer was forthcoming. He was talking to himself really, making a pretty speech, rehearsing as he did sometimes, little effects that might just lure some sign of appreciation from his mother.

"Douris has many alien suggestions. Unlikely suggestions. Concerning deity. Can you predict the next apotheosis of oncoming divinity? What is the chart of your boat's sailing?"

Hedylus let various disjointed sentences trail off across his forehead, rather he visualized them irrelevantly, as being like those fishes on the stair-head where his mother had been jeered at by Irene. For he was sure now (thinking casually back to the early evening) it was mockery that made Irene say, "Moon in half-light, moon in brilliance." This returning to the present gave the same odd effect of some dissociation, exact and only half-sensed reality; the moon (Irene was right) upholding its own shadow in manifest and vibrant crescent. The crescent being only one part, for all appearances. So this. This substance, he maintained, was shadow. The shadow? Mightn't it, by exact reasoning, become more vibrant, more dynamic than the precise reality? Well, he couldn't stand here forever, conjecturing on a shadow. A question would disperse it.

"Can I perhaps help you find the others?"

For perhaps this thing (apparition?) was lost. There was yet possibility that it might be a mortal. "Are you lost simply?"

Words flashed out in answer, words like some soft fur covering a claw pad. A bear's foot was padded softly like a wild-cat's. Hedylus didn't catch the sense, simply felt the shock the suave words brought him. Wild-cat and domestic. Little ferrets on the hillside. Something wild and with claws pointed, yet furred over. So this speech was sharp yet furred over, as it were, by the most sophisticated polished accent. The man (Hedylus had it) talked like Hedyle. Prolonged syllable, pause and blurred-over effect of half-drawled accent, then the sudden swift rending of the veil of words with sharp thought. The thought showed through the casual utterance like pointed claws that must tuck themselves under in order not utterly to destroy the fabric. The spoken words became thin fabric, veiling too sharp thought behind it. The man had said only, "I'm not lost exactly."

There was nothing in what he said, nothing remarkable superficially in the way he said it, yet the words held (it was apparent to Hedylus) some cryptic meaning. *Not lost.* What god was at home now in this chopped-up universe? That seemed to be what the man was driving at. Thought and philosophy had driven the gods from Delphi, all but drained them from Eleusis. Gods now were treated like vermin in low-lying marshes, to be dried out by sterile philosophic speculation or to be drained away like fetid useless water.

The being (apparition?) was not lost. But was he? Hedylus heard the voice continuing, "I mean, I came here prompted by curiosity." Curiosity? What did it hope to find here?

"I was making circuit of the island when I heard you," the voice went on.

"Oh," Hedylus thought, "he heard me speaking; spying

was he? ah"—presentiment flashed across the boy's mind. Maybe this was the common enemy, the astute legate from the mainland, spying out their little island preserve, the exact reliability of their fortress and their material resources. A spy of some subtle order. What a fool he had been! "Douris, my master, I am sure, would be grieved to feel you were neglected," Hedylus said wryly. The figure loomed above him but this was his job simply. The island was the property of Douris. Douris' honour and his kingship had maintained him. Hedylus had been protected by this Douris. "Won't you come up-stairs with me?"

"I think," the voice answered him (familiar Attic accent) "you had better call my boatman." That would be, it was obvious, the more expedient way of getting up-stairs. The bushes loomed above them, the hanging wilderness that was, must be (to the man facing the wall behind him) mysterious barrier. "How do you yourself then come here?" It was obvious that the man was spying for some more material evidence. Wasn't it enough that this stranger had slid in here unannounced and absolutely usurped his privacy? Must he know as well, of the steep ascent from the hillside, the slide upward, crawling like any lizard, that was in its odd way, more dangerous than the slide down? The man had interrupted him, moreover, in his half-unconscious project of that sudden too easily explained slip downward. Now, as Hedylus observed him closely, he could perceive astuteness, intelligence of some unusual order, a bearing that was absolutely not to be mistaken. The man was, it was obvious, some officer, some ex-officer, one of the tribe Douris particularly dreaded. There was always danger of interference, from Asia, from Europe. Europe, on the whole, was the worse because of internal complications. You knew what an Asiatic was up to, at least knew he must be up to something. This sort of frank European was more difficult to cope with.

"I sometimes employ the boatmen. Tonight, I—well, slid around those"—Hedylus pointed vaguely to the left where the rocks were deep in shadow—"boulders."

"Isn't it somewhat difficult?"

"I know the island," the man might as well see what he had to deal with, "and all our visitors."

"O?"

"I mean, precisely, as I at first instance stated, I am sorry to have missed you in the throne-room."

If he were what he seemed to be, the stranger should have been there last night. "Unless you came, as may well be, with—Demetrius." Demetrius. The word after his first insinuation that the man hadn't been received in Douris' last assembly, smote Hedylus edgewise. Demetrius. It brought back Hedyle and the bright chamber and Hedyle stumbling forward. There was a bracelet and its head was lapis. Lapis was bluer than the eyes of Hedyle but held no such pure dimension. The eyes of Hedyle were dew on a blue-lotus. Ice over gentians expressed Irene. They both had those heaven-azure eyes and that odd glamour. Hedyle (it was evident) had died sometime since; Hedylus had realized that when she had said, "Demetrius." Irene wasn't, as was evident, yet born. Hedylus stood between them, part of the past and of the unexpressed future; dead and not-born expressed him. It was obvious the man was just some ordinary person. Perhaps not, after all, dangerous. "You came, then, with Demetrius?"

The boatman (it *was* old Karo) was waiting by the shore-edge. Evidently he had been there some moments, listening. Well, in case of absolute violence, Karo must be on his side. But would he? Hedylus wondered, as Karo became a bronze, lit in the moonlight as by temple torches, as his hand that a moment since had clung to the rough shore-edge, was lifted reverently to draw the robe of the stranger (stepping across the boat-edge) from the water. To Karo, at least, this was some high functionary, but "much," Hedylus thought caustically, "can be done with small coin." Karo always was a fraud and again and again had been summoned for interfering with the servants of legations. Karo must be reprimanded.

"Karo, why did you come here?" The boat had nosed out, plunging through molten silver, moving then like a slim stylus across metal surface. Karo was busy with the oars, didn't perhaps hear him. Didn't want to listen.

"Karo—" but the man cut across that with "I must explain. I was committed by your Tyrant to the little winter-palace; he called it the pavilion."

"O, the pavilion? I lived there with my mother."

Hedyle flashed across him in the man's smile, "your mother?"

"Hedyle, precisely." Now if he were asked his own name, this person would know everything.

My name, my name, my name. What is my name anyway? I am enclosed in Hedylus, the son of Hedyle. Hedyle still encloses me as if I never were born. The boat slid out from the shore, slid across the surface of the metallic water and then sunk as in a second into some other element. "I'm daft, it's obvious." The boat had seemed to slide across a barrier, to slip from an ungracious (for all its beauty) plate of solid metal into a livelier element. Water became something to be worshipped. The old gods matter. Water became the very element that opened to let the earth live. Aphrodite, Aphrogenia had sprung from just such element.

Hedylus, in his acute perception, yet realized that he was thinking elsewhere. Thinking and perceiving, he saw were several elements. He was perceiving this thing. Karo was Karo still, yet Karo had no resemblance to the avid scoundrel, always somehow affectionately condoned since childhood. Karo was an old rogue. Even an old rogue can become a creature of some subtler substance. Once the wine-god took an old rogue for a father. Silenus. There seemed some element of greatness, of enduring truth in Karo. Karo is the same as ever. Hedylus concentrated on this Karo. He didn't dare face the man beside him.

"Maybe, I've slipped out, gone out, am dead simply." His projected idea seemed visibly to have been accepted. Perhaps when we do make up our minds to something, are ready for annihilation, it comes simply. It seemed to Hedylus, facing the old boatman, that he had full open-eyed experience of some after-incarnation. If I had slipped out, though (his thought sustained him) too easily, too readily, without valour and without sustenance, I don't believe they'd want me. *They* seemed suddenly to become visual in his mind, gods and gods and half-gods. It's obvious, he thought, that everyone holds in himself germ of divinity. Mama is Pallas and Aphrodite, mixed and thwarted and struggling side by side within her. Karo is old Silenus. Each is divine but clouded by earth humanity. We are clouded by humanity, bound and tied to earth, being born of earth so clearly. Later... the boat swung toward shore, seemed to slide across a silver mirror.

Hedylus started in the boat-prow. Had he been, then, dreaming? The boat was a pointed stylus sliding over silver. We've come out of the divine element back to every-day things... the man was seated, his head bent forward. Then casually, he motioned Karo to the landing.

KARO UNDID KNOTS, the usual boat-things, gathered oars,

fastened the boat-keel. The voice spoke then, usual furred-over syllables hiding...something other. The man was the earth and the flower sprung from it equally. The man, Hedylus mused, not daring yet to lift his eyes and face the stranger, was (he knew infallibly) fully evolved, the man and the god, each alive, each alert to each contingency. The man was alive, but sheltering the god; the god was sheltering the man. They fitted each other, sword and perfect scabbard. "I see," the boy thought, "in spots, come in and out, creep back to my half-discarded old shell." The man was speaking to him, "won't you come indoors with me?"

"I'd love to," Hedylus was saying, then remembered. "I told you a moment since" (it was years since, another planet since, it was before that sensation of slipping out of life he had had on the live water), "my mother lived here."

Again the man said, "your mother," smiling.

Hedylus cut him with swift gesture, "I claim ancestry from my mother." It was out now. "I am called simply Hedylus."

"Hedylus." Hedylus knew now why the name was adequate. Had he known a father, he had borne some other (towering among men with greatness) high-sounding title. No name, no title, no claim for paternal greatness would answer to his high-strung mind as this did—Hedylus, as the man repeated it. Simply as a string struck, his mind responded to his name as tonic music.

X

HEDYLUS. That is my name, Hedylus. I stand here midway between Hedyle and Irene. Hedyle has already died, Irene isn't yet born. Nevertheless, there confronted him something that showed him in a flash that there was something other than "not born" or "dead already."

He thought starkly, "this mass, this man beside me shows me life so simply." Life was poised, heavy yet gracious on the stone water-steps above him, life tossed silver toward old Karo, life itself was concentrated in eyes facing the cold water, eyes that proved this was a man simply, not merely a statue of a general, some high dignitary symmetrically placed on the stone steps above him. Life moved swiftly in the fling of a cloak-end, and turned aside to let him, Hedylus (a dream simply), stride beside it.

"I've always walked as in a dream, before an invisible amphitheatre." He didn't know if he had said that, spoken it, or merely, in his tense way, thought it. But anyhow, the man would understand. Life would proffer what the gods refused to grant him, understanding and a physical manifestation of omnipotence. He had been a dream, and now, standing under the bare poplar, he saw that he had slid (as one slides from one layer of water into another layer) into life simply. "I seem to have been in a half-state, understanding the dead and the unborn, not understanding anything."

The giant poplar formed an intricate pattern across the imposing outer corridor. The porches were all open, seemingly to sunlight rather than to winter. The sun lay heavy always at this corner; now it was steeped in this peculiar amber-coloured, pollen-dusted moonlight. The moon in a second, would go. Hedylus felt presentiment of this as he said, "can't we get indoors?" There were lights (more than he and his mother had affected in the old days) and voices in the porches. Hedylus thought, "he has his retinue. He must be quite important." Hedylus marvelled that he could even for a moment, have contemplated the man as an adventurer. The stranger, as he moved tactfully forward, seemed so obviously of their world, their convention, astutely understanding apparently each of the corridors, the hidden staircase, the hall.

"The hall-way used to be overcrowded. Mother had all the statues cleared out. They were, she used to assert, of the wrong attributes. Mama used to say she wanted the corridors empty in order to line them with her visions. Mama was always funny." He was speaking with the child-lisp that he had almost grown away from, slight hesitancy in speech, none in thought however. It was perfectly evident that the man had been here, known it intimately. Had he lived here all the time with Hedyle? With Hedylus? The moon can be responsible for apparitions. To see the man in torch-light was yet more astonishing.

"Mama used to say we must remember." Mama. Mother. Hedyle. It was Hedyle, Hedylus felt, had trained him for this moment. Life was preceding him to their own outer chamber.

"Remember?"

"Athens. Certain codes of rightness."

He seemed to have spoken to himself priggishly, spoken to this man as he wouldn't have dared speak to anyone. One didn't, it was obvious, say such things. "Codes of rightness."

That was Hedyle. What was she but incarnate and astute (when you came to think dispassionately of it) rightness, rectitude? In this, the man resembled (as in his odd perfection of accent and affected utterance) Hedyle. Was it Athens simply?

"I mean, I never lived there. Was taken away as a small thing. Never knew it." Had he never? The eyes in the light that might be daylight, showed him what he never had forgotten; as a scene remembered through a wall that's falling, he recalled Athens.

Hedylus said again, this time with no odd feeling that he was falling into blackness, "my mother is Hedyle, the Athenian. You must meet her with me." Curiously now Hedylus, arrogantly proud to claim ancestry only from that mother, repeated, "the Athenian."

Something had lifted, the dream marring his clear perception. What was there to mar him? Life stood here, extravagantly appraising Hedylus. Life, cities, the palace of Demetrius was so much plaster to be swept away by this man's fingers. Hedylus might laugh now, Irene was right. Demetrius was—funny. Life pulsed and had no irony to offer, no stab in the back always. Life fronted him, was friendly, life pulsing in ships, under tent-canvas. Hills. Rocks. Mountains and the torrents falling. Cold water seemed to lie across his forehead. As he faced the stranger, back disaster seemed cleansed; these eyes washed it away like a cold hand disentangling branches from frantic mad eyes. Eyes saw clearly, facing these eyes. Cold water seemed to press light across his forehead. Just such water as must lie inland, in tiny forest lakes, Arcadian lakes such as Irene told him of, set deep in thick moss, lined with tiny dwarf-pines that formed jagged crown. Water reflected wood-flowers, blossom of wild berries. Berries like those in his own secret cavern.

Still facing hypnotic eyes (in his old childhood surroundings), Hedylus thought of distant hills. Reaches of rock. Rock that tilted up...shelf on shelf. Each separated shelf having a separate entity (he had been striving to express that in his poetry), a separate life, an altitude that bred on each fine floor of moss-covered shale a different kind of mountain-growing lily. Lilies. Those were the flowers, that, facing those cold eyes, his heart enquired for. He visualized even rarer blooms than those exotic ones brought overland, from valleys opened by Macedonian Philip's conquests. Philip of Macedonia really was responsible for the exotic spaces of the palace garden, especially for that "blue" terrace that was his mother's terrain. If the Macedonian had not flung his legions east, far and far toward improbable Scythia and beyond legendary India, the very gardens of Samos had been different. Two forces struggled now in Attica. In Greece. In the known plotted world. The south with its burden of incongruous spice and glorious plant that dwarfed to insignificance these of their native villages, the north from which Philip originally had come. Thrace. Further. And in the eyes of the stranger facing him, he read these contradictions.

If eyes could be cold, these were. If volcanic rock should split, showing ice-floe beneath it, this face could be so contrasted. Hedylus thought of the splintered white of a Parian portico. Such frozen grain of marble as he had noted when red field-poppies and warm unfamiliar down-rush from a bruised skull, had so long ago made that dramatic contrast. Ice and fire. Blood and the splintered shale of holy temple-column. In the face opposite him, he traced these elements.

The voice enquired courteously, in familiar Greek of the origin of the author of the poetry. He had then (Hedylus shivered, intellectually relived it), been chanting somewhat lustily those sacred, secret lines, thinking himself in that cavern, of all places, adequately secreted.

He said, "I wrote the things. " There seemed no reason for denial as he faced those eyes that burnt almost white in their curious penetrating greyness; white, if eyes could be white, concentrated, phosphorescent. "You listened then?"

"I could not help hearing, as I drifted toward the mainland. I was tired of the distinct trivialities about us."

"You were with the party up-stairs?"

"Douris had asked me; left word for us here, at this very villa. We arrived yesterday."

"I see. I missed you last night in the throne-room."

Hedylus realized that he had said this before but he repeated the set formula out of some renewed sense of respect for an outworn convention. He heard answer as conventional.

"For myself, discourtesy claims that I failed you."

"Douris' little assemblies become boringly inadequate."

"The island provinces amuse me."

"You have been long wandering?"

"Some years, furtively."

"Furtively?"

"Work, commissions connected with overland caravans."

"You are Asiatic?"

"All influenced Greece is that."

All this. Listening, Hedylus raised high (as he felt forever now he must do), his bruised forehead, and stood, young courtier, now with renewed old convention (intellectually reawakened), slightly cynically on guard, at polite attention; he heard his voice and the answering syllables as he had for singularly monotonous years, been hearing it with selfsame answers in Douris' crowded throne-room. The voice (his own), it appeared, spoke automatically and Hedylus moved with affectation of hauteur a little to one side, half-interested, dispassionately refusing further show of curiosity, and remarked, simply, "that island-side is scarcely made for visitors."

"So I judged, hearing your terse hexameters."

Hexameters. The word jolted from him obvious externals. The very syllables as the man uttered them brought flame of memory. "Hexameters" became live things, rose and writhed and mouthed serpent-jeerings at him. Every word the man uttered seemed indeed "winged," flew out, having body and visible dimension.

Hedylus stammered, "I mean—I did think I was adequately sheltered."

"Sheltered?" Sheltered? What had he meant by sheltered?

"You were never sheltered." Hedylus saw the face and the beauty of the deity of Delphi. *King, lord of the other-world's white ivory portal*, his own words rose to mouth their innate wisdom at him. Words *were* serpents, each one having visible dimension. He had flung words heavenward and not content with his own histrionics, had made suitable altar of flat stones so that smoke curling upward should reach any deity who regarded, meagrely attentive. God had been summoned and God ironically had answered. *I have myself, the azure heaven has no, no heart to doubt you* lingered in memory.

Words that had been so much blue smoke curled upwards, rose out of memory to defy the wan creator. *I sing not as a priest of other-times, but this scroll of small worth contains you*. Wasn't he just the scroll written over and over with bright letters, the parchment that divinity now saw fit to unroll before him? It seemed to Hedylus that the man unrolled him like some written parchment.

"Your writing has only half expressed you."

"My writing?"

"One sees the struggle of some innate force. It breaks out at brief interval."

Hedylus prayed that those ironic syllables would not paw and torture his immature mouse-utterance. The voice, purring like a great cat, rolled out its curious challenge, *"It holds you as the poppy the bright dream, the reed the river."* The man's words had taken out of his own mind the half-formed broken, chopped verse. *"I have no other offering,"* the suave voice continued. It seemed there was ripple as of high-toned laughter. Hedyle's voice (his own voice) flung out, wild, hysterical. Hedylus flung himself face downward on the low couch. His eyes, wide open, seemed to plunge down and down into the dark silk of the cushion covering. His eyes, pressed tight against the regal cushion, seemed to well deep waters and out of water (living water), a face peered ironically. A face seemed to answer his long-unspoken prayer. *Luminous, hear.*

> Luminous,
> hear;
> in other lands
> wan limbs
> and stricken
> hailed you
> and proclaimed you
> master of healing,
> Paeon;
> as of yore,
> see,
> see
> my hands uplifted
> to implore
> your bounty.

One never could, Hedylus discovered, destroy beauty. His lines (destroyed?) were written in his scalding forehead. A voice nearer than his own voice, ringing in memory in his closed brain, whispered, "let me help you."

XI

HEDYLUS KNEW NOW, seated calmly by this stranger, that
he had always been striving self with self, the two distinct halves, reft (he visualized it) that day when at five he
had flung forward, clinging to scrub-root of dwarf-cypress to
find his brow wreathed with poppy-scarlet. That scarlet,
field-flower purple, had been always in his mind, the direct
physical manifestation of his spiritual cleavage. But, strange-
ly, now for the first time in consciousness, he recognized a
subtle difference. Seated on a low couch, his head leaning
against a fold of drapery, he realized at last that his head was
somehow adequately and suitably at one with the length of
thin yet wiry, muscular young torso.

The creature opposite, his heavy body bent somewhat
forward, rested in the old familiar claw-footed chair, model-
led, Hedylus remembered, on archaic pattern. That particular chair was relic of past archaistic fashion and had been
rescued along with various long couches, tables, pedestals,
that had been thought unsuitable by Douris for the palace
proper. The villa, Hedylus recalled, had been, on Hedyle's
expressed wish, almost entirely furnished from slightly
démodé bits of rare and sometimes curious furniture. The
figure seemed seated suitably on some informal throne.

Even now, in the light of fresh lamps, just brought in by

close-cropped, military servants, the stranger opposite defied close observation. Was it, Hedylus pondered, the very passion of his desire that was so thwarting him? For should he stare, open-eyed, full at the apparition, might it not vanish? Or conversely, should he stare wide-eyed at the apparition, might it not, more likely, simply present itself as the most formal of ambassadors, some Greek of the north, some familiar military delegate from Scythia? He knew from long familiarity, the various types, could cope, manage several dialects. Hedylus, Douris had often told him, had in him the making of some diplomatic legate. But should he let his tired eyes properly focus on the person opposite, should he once more summon suavity and mundanity to his rescue (his recent experiment in frigid converse had not wholly pleased him), he might easily, he foresaw, loose both god and champion.

A looseness of entire being. He attributed it to his fatigue, to his paralyzing desire recently, his almost formed project of a careless scramble up the almost impassable cliff-edge and some sub-conscious trail backward, where hands, only half-willing, should clutch at crumbling earth while waxberries and curiously flowering branches should break together beneath lacerated fingers. Half consciously, Hedylus realized what he had half-hoped for. He had visualized the fall, precipitate on to a solid surface, as escape from himself —his blinding forehead—unto . . . something other. The sea in its lapis regularity would, he had felt certain, have shattered him as an unfledged bird fallen wingless from a precipice. And afterwards? He seemed to sense that "something other" near him . . . eyes closed, a sense of well-being, a semi-obscure realization that behind those curtains of dark lids was rose-flame of shaded alabaster. That opposite was such a presence as young Hylas might have dreamed of.

"Your imagery was excellent." The voice, courteous, low-toned, continued dissertation on the poetry. Hadn't

Hedylus (Hedylus thought) already enough suffered in the first encounter? Hadn't he enough proved to this god or being his indifference to mere poetry? "Which imagery?" knowing entirely what it was the man referred to.

"Poems. Your own. The general emotional intensity is excelled only, in my mind, by the vivid and exact presentation of outward condition. The rose unequalled by the cliff-orchid, is a new simile. Flowers in the East enter more readily into the general format of verses. Here, even in our lighter poetry, there is a general striving, a reworking of constant ancient simile. The association in time, becomes monotonous. Even Sappho, most daring and belligerent of rebels, introduces but one (am I not right?) new flower into her verses. If even so, we may strictly term the slight and scentless gold-pulse of the Asiatic islands a true blossom. Your idea of the rock-ridge becoming redivided into separate efflorescence, according to the altitude, implying, as I judge, a spiritual comparison as well as a mere natural one, is unique, differing in all particulars from anything I have yet met with. Combining as it does the stark rock-quality of Attica with the suavity, the ingenuous sweetness of some Carian wild-flower."

"My idea, indigenous to this rock-land, is yet most unoriginal in outline." Hedylus paused. Had he really declaimed that poem on the headland? Dare he presume yet further on the man's autocracy? Should he lie outright, the seated deity that faced him must, in all courtesy, respect his reticence. "The very poem you speak of was in part (though I said I wrote it), recorded from a Syrian manuscript. My patron, Douris of Samos, has expert secretaries skilled in the latest subtleties of lettering and in permanent fixing of rare parchment. They lack, all somewhat, the finer subtleties of artistic honour. Meaning simply that the Tyrant, wishing from time to time to savour in seclusion certain fine lines, before spreading them broadcast where any petty poetaster may take credit for them (by the simple expedient of dressing the old matter in a fresh and somewhat erratic metre), on certain occasion delegates me, a friend, son of his companion Hedyle, to copy for him."

The somewhat elaborate manner of his speech gave him time, while his tongue formed the syllables, to reconsider. To think deftly. Facing him was somewhat of another century. For truly it seemed a sort of courteous Helios had taken modest bearing. This might not or might be god. The slight suggestion of a smile infinitely subtletized the fine lips of the being opposite. Then he spoke softly, almost an affectation of over-breath such as Hedyle at her most impressive moments would indulge in, "and Irene?"

"The name, meaning as it does, some sort of state, mystical almost, of innate quietude (peace, is it?), seemed, has seemed fitting as a sort of dedicatory Muse or presence acclaimed before beginning the more solid matter of the subject—" Hedylus fumbled. The courtesy of the whimsical smile faded. Something (white lightning splintered on some Parian pediment?) flamed steady, till the man opposite seemed veritable marble; it was impossible that the servant moving solid, military, to draw the heavy purple that slung from pillar to pillar (the wind threatened the light from the floating wicks of hemp cloth) caught any hint of what flame, ice-splintered, had assailed him.

Hedylus noted irrelevantly, those wicks were such as seamen burn, as sailors set in bowls on the folding lathes of soft manageable tripods. He noticed further, as he shifted his posture on the low couch, that there was about the casual furnishing of the place still further hint of the wanderer in Asiatic provinces. A pelt lay opposite by the table, across which was stretched an embroidery unfamiliar to him. Flowers of some pointed tongue, twisted martagon-like, tongue of gold and purple threading. The knotted fringe of the very drapery he leaned against held, as he fingered it in his confusion, some strange element, rarer even than the mere lapis smoothness, the soft glaze of his mother's latest iridescent import.

"That—that animal," Hedylus spoke now faltering almost as a child, unexpectedly forgetting the apt form and fluency of the familiar Greek, "is it perhaps some wild-bear?"

"I found it seeking the outskirts of our camp for provender. My men shot pheasant, heavier wild-fowl, duck, and partridge. The creature, with all its suavity of bearing, was somewhat a clumsy hunter. It had crept inland, I presumed perhaps from some ice-ledge; some home of snow surely only could be responsible for that thick marking. We tamed it with refuse, claws, wings, feathers which it tortured, red and peacock-gold, blue and violet against the sweep of winter. I do not think it is a bear. We classified it in our notes as Indian wild-cat, hibernaceous, with its winter white coat."

"It lived then?"

"Some months with us."

"You write?"

"We make notes, plans for campaign, future voyaging."

XII

IT WAS OBVIOUS, closing his tired eyes, the man was god.
Such imagery assailed him. As if by some process of
thought-transference, the man's mind, his voyagings and
discoveries, his very personal outlook were some open script.
Before his closed eyes, Hedylus read as from some stiff and
unfamiliar and totally fascinating manuscript, stories such as
Herodotus (fabulous traveller) might speak of . . . in a sort of
rose-haze which was, he realized, the light permeating his
closed lids from a lamp's familiar alabaster.

That particular flat bowl, set high on the elegant,
somewhat old-fashioned table, reminded him of past talks
with his mother. The very table, too, was awkwardly
familiar. When there was no lamp there (he recalled precisely), it was set inevitably with wild-flowers. Flowers from
the small inland pool, those scarce and rarely to be
discovered water-lilies. Lilies (in his thought) were all about
him. Purple, martagon twist of flame-embroidery, tongue of
citron-yellow, such lilies as Irene told him grew spotted like
moth-wings in Arcadia, lilies of precious form and pattern,
scroll-like on Ionic volute; white lilies brought from Africa,
tended (so priceless) in wet moss though the ranged rowers
dropped, at the last, dead of lingering thirst, such precious
mystic flower, for which men had fallen backward that they,

more suave, more delicate might be placed stiff with fragrant petal in Hedyle's frail fingers. Freesias. Wrapped in cold moss though rowers died for it. Blue wood-lily. The wine-coloured single violet-shaped, acanthus-leaved spear of blossom they had brought from Lydia, the small valley-lily, growing a white spar against a heavy water-lily-like blade of foliage, the simple yellow lemon-lily, the famous, not wholly beautiful orchid-lily with its lavender, marked like some pale butterfly, the soul, the very visible embodiment of beauty. Last and most poignantly, the white shaft that was simply the Greek lily of the islands.

XIII

FACING THE FAMILIAR TABLE that they (Hedylus and Hedyle) had relegated as impracticable for ordinary purposes, and used always as altar for their blossoms, he closed his eyes and again let alabaster light sift through the thin barrier of weary lids. His eyes, blue lilies, seemed closed in by tired eyelids, as some flower by outer foliage. Subconscious and conscious vaguely blurred in him, yet merged, making that smooth stretch of forehead a fine cup, fit for the retaining of intoxicant, almost too heady yet valiantly (for the moment anyhow) kept subservient. Where formerly (some half-hour, was it?) Hedylus had striven half with half, continually readjusting, explaining, as it were, in secret, the motives of himself to this other self that was equally himself, he seemed now to have been made, by the mere physical or spiritual emanation of the man beside him, one entire and concrete entity. Self met self as two waves, for long chafing at some fragile sand barrier, finally join, white with white crest; irradiating a fine spray that told, in an exact moment, that the tiny demarcation of dividing sand (dividing self) was merged, submerged in one wave-length of silver. Cold. Hedylus recognized the exact moment when the old cleft was healed and each self satisfied.

"It would be banal to presume that you might be my

father." The flash answering his smile told him that no claim of mere physical fatherhood could make for such poignancy of understanding. It struck him again that some weight had lifted. Men should, do laugh naturally at things that for him had been for many years, such ill-defined and chafing phobia. Fear striking, grappling, seizing him unaware midnights, so that, even as a small child, he had lain in black sweat till dawn told him no pirate of the mainland, no sorcerer of Crete, could land unannounced and claim him. Hedyle had told him, half suspecting vague disquietude, that by Greek law she only had full power of him. There were, he knew, even in infancy, laws other and differing from the mere law of matter. Hedyle, he saw carefully to it from the first, must not suspect him of these terrors. Guarding her, he fought doubly with his manias. Depression (such as reached, this very afternoon, suicidal climax) was familiar to him. Black waves rose, drowning him; terror estranging him from the small circle of his contemporaries (he had never confided even to Sikeledes), now stood far off. He recognized, dared face inhibition wholly in the light of the white splintered on white marble that was this man's controlled and vibrant being.

"Nights, you know." Hedylus spoke in the voice in which he had a moment since recognized recrudescence of child softness and throatiness, when speaking of the pelt lying at the base of alabaster. He heard a voice (his own) that reminded him of childhood. Not so much the resonant tone (in its deep youthful insistencies of maturity) but the very accent. Those quaint splintered consonants, a legacy from his half-European peasant nurse (Lyda's manner of speech had always quaintly charmed him) and vowels blurred over like water running slow and sullen yet with persistent music, as it does through wood-troughs set on the ridges of farm-lands for the fowl and the shorn sheep to water in at noon. Such sound (half song) recurred, he noted unexpectedly after years' absence, in his accent.

"Hedyle was never with me." He shrugged. Even in childhood he had resented bitterly this absence. "Well, courtesy be due him. Douris has proved excellent in all worldly matters. Mother saw strictly to it. What I chiefly resented with her was the mere fact of her loyalty. She said, had Douris not fancied us, we should have now been starving, burnt-black Alexandrian beggars. We were on our way there. Perhaps that's why she even now, loathes the name of Alexandria. Naturally, too, because of its connection with that (as she called him) scoundrel. She said, after the Macedonian inroads, Athens was unbearable."

"Naturally," the voice asserted, "after great wars, there must be social and political upheaval."

"Not just that. Some secret thwarted her, made her in some way bitter. That bitterness I myself refused to recognize till lately."

The forward bend of the shoulders. The very human quality of interest. The face bronzed a little, now that he scanned it closely. The hair thinning slightly. The heavy and commanding beauty of the chin. The throat rising like a strong gnarled, weathered bronze stalk of fruiting olive; the passivity, the receptivity; the hand resting as it might on the pommel of some great steed; the forehead (he returned to it), Hedylus saw now with the rimmed shadow that was the mark of the helmet's chafing; the knees bare with the heavy military tunic; the legs heavy with neat beautifully bound straps of the thick sandals; the heavy marks again defining, below the knees, the chafing occasioned by the rub and scar of heavy leather or of wrought metal; the folds of the tunic; again the chin, out-thrust like some ironic and commanding deity. Behind him, Hedylus sensed an unassailable beauty as of gull-wings.

Hermes. Sandals and winged helmet. No. Hermes would not fit this. Helios, architect, leader of the colonists. Helios, father of the lost Ion, father of small Aesculapius, lover and ravisher of Daphne, slayer (indirectly) of tall Hyacinth. Helios, lover, founder of far city, colonizer. Wearing shield, helmet if need be, greaves if necessary (yet no Ares), lord of swift steeds, purveyor for Greece of music from Asiatic fastness, lover of the singing Muses. Irene. Following his own thought, Hedylus said, "it seems to me always, in pursuing Attic legend, that Helios was least fortunate."

The upper lip was, Hedylus noted, caught in, giving the taut chin a flattened outline. The brow held distinctly a furrow, and pain (that swept scorching) was betrayed by that mouth outline. The eyes caught his to themselves as some desert-scorched plateau may drink in blue rain-water. Hedylus caught the fringe of the rich cloth; confusion dulled him in a moment. "Least," he repeated, gaining full strength to face the other opposite, "of the deities to be envied." The face was still exposed in its fire of white pain, but the suave voice answered, unexpectedly unemotional, "the most perhaps, unfortunate. But playing large stakes. Adventurous. Lovable, somewhat." The stranger spoke, impersonal, as if he were not that god. "Somewhat impressionable." Hedylus felt now he was lost, as a runnel from some cold snow-bank that has been adequately absorbed into a larger bed of low-lying, heavier water. He was lost, melted, like snow melted into water that holds perhaps deposit of experience, in-drifted silt; he was snow, too soon scorched to nothingness. Helios in that was, it appeared, unfortunate.

The man unmoving had betrayed his godhead. This was the manner with him. Helios at the moment of embracing Daphne, burnt her with like fire. Helios as he stood simply noting the forward-flung sway of youthful muscle and the rhythmic swing of fine-muscled bodies, had even in that glance betrayed himself. The wind flinging a bright disc forward had struck young Hyacinth. Helios was always fated to hold in his arms dead, exhausted embers of humanity.

This doubt mocked Hedylus. A moment since, it seemed his head had been filled with rare intoxicant and he the master of it. Doubt now seared him. His thought had been white wine, flecked with fine amber and electric fire-spark. Yet controlled, aptly. Now fear entered that head which had been a cold chased goblet in which thought flickered, as light caught on white wine; clear thought and cold like sunlight on white grapes. His thought, Hedylus reviewed it in a flash of vague presentiment, had been that. Pure marble would have seemed drab beside the flow and interplay of light, beside the intoxicant that his skull had then contained. Now, somewhat, he was threatened.

Helios, it was obvious, was again caught open-handed. Did he always, thus flinging earthward his great and holy effulgent presence, find himself rejected? No, not rejected. It was only that men could not, dared not accept the unveiled presence. Hedylus felt the old pain that was again bound tight, child poppy-crown of martyrdom. Was he falling? Would he fall? The man's lifted hand suddenly challenged his infirmity. He straightened. "My work. This afternoon. It was nothing, yet I loved it. Irene and my mother quarrel. Irene is a quaint girl. She hates weaving, stitching, embroidery. Women hate her. At least do not ever want her. She says men likewise. She at least fears them. My friend, the poet Sikeledes, would love to champion her. She repudiates all help. Her boat leaves Samos shortly. Her father, ambassador from the Peloponnesus, takes her with him. Unless Sikeledes could keep her. But would he ever understand her? Do men always break a woman who is perfect? Child-bearing, I am certain, is some whim of cruel divinity. Can nothing alter such things?"

His lids parted. Black, suggesting stormy child-torment

of weeping, rimmed his white lids. Great scars like the inner heart of the blood-and-flame ember of the field-flower. His stormy sorrow was salt-whipped gull-fastness, shut apart from human probing, shut away, apart from human curiosity. "My mother had some sorrow bearing me. For fun, I used to say the gods had ravished Hedyle. Beauty is, for the innocent, misfortune." This, now controlled, he swiftly contradicted.

"Not that. She is no common woman. You will see her. She is perfect, yet somewhat too finely intellectual. A woman should be, but rarely can achieve it. At least, having that mark set straight upon her forehead, she should (in this the poets show, as in most incidence, their inner vision) abstain from mortal commerce. Athené, full-armed, should give no favour. Virgin, tried substance of deity. Pure mind should be balanced and unmated. Herself, forward reaching patron of youth, lover of all industry, should be unwedded. Pallas ravished by the sun-god would have such a child as I am." Thus speaking, tense intake of breath, swift passionate outbreathing, left him empty, vacant as some runner stumbling forward, outdistanced now, certain of defeat. "Finding you as I have, I must tell you you have helped me." Hedylus sat now quiet, somewhat less severe; in his white face the ice-flower blue reclaimed (as dawn in some hill-valley) day from blackness. He smiled even, his mouth in its simple line, unimpassionate, "so I want to help Irene."

"The girl I saw padding about (was it two mornings since, when the boat landed?) with tangled fish-nets dragged from small, clenched, incompetent, tight hands?" It was exact Irene. The curious slouch-forward that was her not wholly gracious movement, her tiny hands, improbably fine, delicate as some delicate, awkward flower-bud. Hands, delicate, with a fineness of texture that might well cause Hedyle apprehension; Hedyle with claw-like, exquisite, electrically intellectualized fine fingers. Hedyle's fingers were deft, swift in tearing movement, giving vision of some bird-claw, rapacious, again subtilized almost to some impossible sensitivity. Pallas would have, did, does have such hands as Hedyle. The others, the small hands of Irene, incongruously attached to that boyish, unimpressionable stolidity were small, tight infolded, utterly useless and unfitted to her mind's brave projects. Exactly this man had seen (flashing at Hedylus a smile composed now, slightly humorous) Irene.

"She does pad somewhat." Again Hedylus felt some curious crinkling of eyes, some curious peeling-off, as it were, of his stern fixity of thoughtful, grave expression. "She isn't, you can see, like others. I don't know what she wants quite. She herself doesn't know that either. Only like me she gets strange phobia. Fear obsessions. That's why she's always busy. So she can't think about it. I don't know that she'll do it."

The man again seemed utterly human. He wasn't (this was a great discovery) at all godlike. "Do what exactly?"

"O, she has various different reasons for it. She thinks sheer drowning would accomplish, bring some consummation. I don't know. I say yes, do by all means, only isn't it, don't you think, a little unwise of Irene? I mean so singularly to set her disapproval of the whole of outer loveliness, to set, as it were, her seal of negation on the whole of life, to thus assert the whole wine-cask is one turgid mass of dead lees, before she has (as is evident) not so much as set lip to the wine-cup. I myself wouldn't give in to her, only I understand, though for myself I should prefer some swift falling from a high place. Sudden, violent, shattering rather than the prolonged strangulation, the suffocation of sheer drowning. I tell her these things.

"Posidippus, my other friend, of course attempted loving. She hates him for it. She says now she is just a boy.

Which of course she plainly isn't." Hedylus saw the net tangled, the utter Gordian knot that was Irene's problem. "Sikeledes, dear fellow, is no lover for her. His poems (you know them?) exquisite. But I feel they wear the stamp of some too inviolate inhumanity. A person like Sikeledes must love some large mature blossom of a woman. Some exuberant creature. At once melting and merging with her, he would cast off, as in some spiritual process of elimination, his fine verses. To, if you will, some such unattainable and awkward spirit as Irene. But close contact with Irene would only thwart, baffle, and depress him. Close contact with Irene would make him finally a sullen, uninventive poet. As it is, as it might well be, some flower of obvious soft maturity would free him."

The head, forward bent as if some wise philosopher sat there detached, wholly sympathising, wholly seeing, wholly and utterly comprehending. The white flame gone, the man was obviously and, O so beautifully, nothing, no one, just as was fitting, one of the ambassadors that so often dropped (didn't Hedylus know the whole gamut of them?) from Asia to Europe, from Europe back to Asia. Ever since he could remember anything, he recalled those crowded throne-rooms where he, as a small boy even, was drawn close into the circle, the inner ring where Hedyle sat close to Douris in blue imperishable loveliness.

There was Hedyle first, of course, but speaking of Irene, some arid thirst was quenched as with water from an Arcadian rivulet. He apprehended, as it were, small berries and tiny low-growing, star-shaped deep rose and shell-lavender florets, resting on stiff moss-like evergreen foliage. Pools where tiny fish glinted, splinters of smooth grey and shining agate. Small waters where one could adequately define one's self, with which one might adequately measure one's possibilities.

"She says she thinks she is some wild sea-creature. Fishing. Pulling in nets. Always with the men about the islets. She fancies she is violently masculine. You saw her fingers." Their eyes met. "The tiny childlike hands, so unfitting to the brave sea-faring mentality of the child. She is so tiny. And her mind, violent, instructive, deep and plausible. She seems to be always a sort of Muse, rather than any goddess, or any god's child. Clio. Some frantic and intense desire for knowledge. Hedyle, like Pallas, is swift in her exact and patent formula. Little Irene is Clio, more one of the circle that enchant the sun-god."

How could he ever have mistaken this mere stranger? Hedylus saw the very crease and fleck of sun-burnt skin, a little wrinkled humanly at the eyes; the under-lip a bit arrogantly and a little cruelly out-thrust; the hand coarsened by weather, resting heavy on his knee; the fingers slightly blunted, heavy somewhat, the knees with the coarse fibre of slightly disproportioned heavily weathered muscle; again the eyes set back, veiled now to commonplaceness; the nose straight but a little darkly heavy. The man said, "why don't you try petting her a little?"

"It is of course the obvious solution. But I don't know quite." Hedylus humanly faced his interlocutor. He did know. He did quite know why the obvious was not the expedient. "I remember, of course, always her fox-fury (tiny threatened quarry) with Posidippus, who had, after all, fluency, gallantry, charm, technique to put it bluntly. Posidippus, always somewhat wary yet not at all narrow in his tastes, was if any, I should have thought, the person for her."

Still the eyes opposite. And in the rose of shaded alabaster, Hedylus felt old premonition, familiar shivering such as he had long associated with evenings with his mother, before dining, when she sat low, grey in an undefined blurr of frightening shadow, crouched forward somewhat on the lion-footed couch.

"Evenings bring cold stark fear. I spend them with my mother." This obviously was no excuse.

"Your *mother?*"

"Hedyle," Hedylus pronounced it as always with an unconscious stiffening, a straightening of posture, offering this as always, as the final explanation of all things, "demands much of me; time; all I have of power."

He recalled that eternal slogan that had been, some years since, branded indelibly. Hedyle had so often told him (he couldn't help constantly remembering), lacking Douris, they had long since been outcasts, beggars in some dark slum.

"My mind, such as it is—" Wings seemed beating back of him . . . in the rose of the shaded alabaster. Strength that was made assuredly, from the beginning, for a child to rest on. From the first, he had been denied it. Wings beating back of the head, bent forward, ironic with set smile, with set impassivity, seemed to speak of something finer than Athenian intellect. This "something other" that he from the first sensed as the aim really and end of all super-subtilization of fine intellect. That "something other" must come through the mind's portal as through fine ivory pillars. Illumination would never come to an Athenian (for he was, after all, that) otherwise.

Wings beating and fear such as Hyacinth apprehended when the god glanced at him. Too fine, too rare, he might, reasonably now that he was welded into one piece (now that his mind had cast aside the fine ache of passionate speculation) break. Paeon having so obviously healed him, it was, he saw it, in this man's power to break; to speak one slight word, to move hypnotically his arm upward, or to swerve by so much as hairbreadth, his head backward, to nod conceivably forward, and in a manner that had nothing to do with thought, that superseded mere thinking as the blossom burst from the fine glazed calyx may exceed (in beauty and in fire) that carefully fitted and fine finished leafage, so this that superseded thinking might entrap him.

The servant entering, answered the soft oriental clap-clap that was his master's signal. Spread in no appreciable time, with the slightest amount of movement, with apparently no sound at all, a low unfolding table. Set thereon mechanically bowls, plates, while with no movement, with no appreciable change of atmosphere, the stranger, with that affectation of stressed syllables that was reminiscent of Hedyle's sophisticated utterance, stated simply, "you will," with the least possible upward inflection that implied that there was (as there so obviously was not) choice left to him, power of refusal, "dine with me?"

XIV

"IF," Hedylus said, as he held the chill metal cup child-like, in long hands and turned it round and round, gazing spell-bound into its glinting centre, "Irene would let go somewhat."

"There are," the man answered, "means, methods, wine, for instance, the gods' beatifier."

"Ah, really, I have tried it."

But how enter further into Irene's complicated psychology? Hadn't he for these weary months, from that first marked day he had met her (winter-rain he remembered, had smitten the first premature exquisite almond-branches) thought of nothing else? Gazing, hypnotized, into the glinting rim of the cup that shone up at him like some new and unfamiliar planet-curve, Hedylus wanted poignantly, obstinately, to betray Irene. Tyranny such as she exerts is, taken all in all, he pondered, worse far than the fiery impulsive, passionately overbearing maternal tyranny of these Hedyles. Hedyle's tyranny had to be tolerated. There were excuses for her. One must make allowances for the situation, the never-to-be-solved problem of a child, a single child born secretly and, as in his case, unlawfully.

"That alters everything." Following his own thought, he found he must explain it. "My birthright. She started conscientiously to do for me. She might, mightn't she, have easily deserted me? She has used this fitfully. But just lately it has seemed (finding her hectic and unpolished and unreasonable) that Douris bores her. She might, long ago, have left him for another."

"Presumably. But is not a woman of what obviously must be your mother's temper (the man used the word as one speaks of a steel blade) "open to this conclusion: having tasted out of the lawful régime of the humdrum, all men must be alike dullards. The mind, flaming a little above the body proper, seeks other outlets."

This reasoning, Hedylus could frankly follow. Lifting his head with its scar, its thick chaplet of dark hair, its chin cleft as if some very archaistic chisel had been set there, with its straight yet slightly broadened, a little thickened nostrils, with above that not too perfect modelling, the drawn and exquisitely perfected burnt-black eyebrows, with (beneath those wing-curves that were a very swallow for uptipped wing-flight) eyes that were blue, though heavy pupil gave them a curious darkness, he was, Hedylus himself realized, apt pupil for some necromancer. *The mind seeks other outlets.*

Necromancer. Magician. Delphian rocks held imprint of fingers that had trailed careless garments, outgrown of him, of a little too coarse texture for the fire that was his man flesh. Garment of laurel, rose like shaded alabaster. About the boy there was that curious inner light like the light hyacinths seem curiously to give out when bred in certain earth strata. Hyacinths that glow as if some transcendental fire were set within, out-glowing like these wicks (he recognized as part of seaman's, of soldier's outfit) burning low in sweet-oil.

Conceivably. Music, the dance, poetry even, any matter having to do with sculpture. Hedylus knew the stranger had no thought of these things. But should he let go now firm hold on things of intellect, he was charmed past sure recovery. For mightn't this creature, after all, be some cruel demon, about to take one up, so to speak sheltering, later to let one, like young Hylas, fall down, like some burnt-out meteor, to some abyss of inconceivable blackness?

Hedylus saw swiftly, with intuition bred of constant intercourse with the tyrannous, exacting, and super-sophisticated Hedyle, what all this might mean. Give up Douris and his small hold on the court-circle, his slight yet definitive position, his possibilities of artistic recognition, of moving in a small poetic circle with two adequately matched friends, Posidippus, Sikeledes. Friendship even such as Sikeledes had offered him, would do no good here. It was, it might be, a pre-natal distrust of all men. He could tell no one of it. Ah, possibly Irene.

"These fruits this year are a little bitter-seasoned." The serving-men had taken away dish and heavy goblet; set on the spread cloth, silver and flasks so thin that light seemed almost to show through metal surface. Hedylus lifted a heavy fruit of grape. The white berries seemed over-weighted in that light, like heavy crystal drops elongated at the tip, about to drop down by very surfeit.

"Conditions of sun and wind. But we always have them." In his voice he recognized a weary overtone. Such passion, again in that sudden intuition, he realized, to be sustained, would require some godlike substance, some Herculean power, something dark and wholly substantiated like dark earth-crust of upward towering mountain.

"We are expert in gardening. What time can be spared her from her blue-flower terrace, my mother herself spends in the vineyards. We have a small in-sheltered space where exact Homeric conditions always reign. We have berries like these, growing beside the green-grape and between them both, the separating delicate tendril of the spice-green flower."

Head forward bent, those eyes that were, he recognized, stormy themselves with hopelessness. But adequate; an autocrat. Hedylus feared too much to yield, too terribly he feared lest by some mischance this man (god to him) should feel him unperceptive.

"But Irene. She is some tiny Aphrodite, rose-petal of some low-growing wax-flower, as I have written. In my songs I dare utterly to reveal her. Sikeledes, more adequate, has not, I am sure of this, the right image. To him, she is some strange, wayward creature. She is not, really. She is small, domestic, curiously deliberate and child-like. I can't rescue her."

"But she—why not let her do the rescue?" He had not so far thought this. Now in a moment, as he broke the last of the crystal berries, Hedylus realized the inner reading of his champion.

"You mean one's self? Throw, so to speak, one's weakness at her?"

"Hadn't you thought of it?"

"It never entered into my calculation."

"I see."

"Really to help her, I must let her help me?"

XV

B UT THAT WAS NOT THE POINT, that was not the point really. What really mattered was just this. Small wax-floret, tiny and exquisite undergrowth of dwarf-arbutus, of virgin, cold and child-like wood-anemone (not the great rose and purple and frayed lavender and ivory flower-cups, but the tiny frost-delicate wood-flower) frost anemone, tiny wax-floret of evergreen leafage, pink arbutus, that was all Irene. But over it, he perceived (as a flung garment) the whole of the laurel that must crown Parnassus. Giant bush, beneath which he would find adequate shelter, beneath which he would be fittingly obliterated. Rose and purple heads of great flower that grow close on heavy budlike calyx to the wood-fibre of the great bush. Laurel-bush and tree which would dwarf to insignificance one such small Irene.

He saw this, his head no longer aching with the old familiar mental striving, but with a darker turmoil; a crack indeed had been healed, a fissure from which, so recently, blue smoke-like thought pulsed upward. To Irene, his poems in the cliff side. But what poems, should he adequately strive, might be to the deity forthcoming? His mother had perhaps been right. "O child, if you hadn't broken your head, you'd be another Sophocles."

Had Sophocles, Euripides, the whole gamut of them,

seen what he had? Sitting unimpassioned apparently, with fine metal (an unfamiliar planet-rim) turning in hands that mechanically turned and turned, giving full space of conscious attention to the thing opposite, the man with the wine-cup resting on the table, with quiet fingers. Fingers; fingers. Hedylus felt, in that inconsiderable moment, the vast difference in them. And it was (wasn't it?) just that difference that made the task more painful? Let go; spark of electric fire would answer spark of fire. But how intense, he had no way of gauging. Only he felt, with an intuition bred by long slavery to Hedyle's over-sophisticated intellect, that there would be, must be, final severence. And once having merged with this, what spiritual death would attend such parting?

"I'd come with you," he spoke, listening astonished to a colourless utterance, "to India," for hadn't the man (it seemed incredible) just asked him, "be, as you suggest, your secretary. Draw your maps, outline your discoveries, collect and arrange your flowers, help hunt your animals." He felt the other knew what fire drained animation from his thin speech. He must, could scarce help realizing. "I'd love to come." Hedylus felt the old quaver, almost as if some long stifled nervous child-wail must break forth. Shame him, disprove his brave mentality.

He felt, standing by the purple curtain, now making his adieus, some terrible and stark reminder. In the folds of just this purple, he had played at Circe, at Crete, at the tip of Sparta that was one enormous emerald, too heavy for Hedyle's frail forearm. Two great uneven green stones. His hand was raised, ready to part the curtain. He remembered years spent, in the folds of just this purple, watching, guarding, sheltering Hedyle.

"I'd ask you to the villa. Ours. To see Hedyle."

The man too was standing, a little too easily, his hand resting on his great chair, his mouth drawn, in a whimsical ironic smile, and he answered, blithely, swiftly, with a flash of decorous politeness, overdone by just that slight drawback of the smile that showed cruel now, bitter, "I should be charmed to see—Hedyle."

Like a knife trained in passage of Eastern sword-play, yet all the time irrevocably Greek, he said "Hedyle."

Hedylus just repeated that "Hedyle." Then turning, he stumbled down the shallow stairs into the familiar garden, realizing the enormous unsubstantiated square of light was just the curtains parted, held wide by some invisible attendant, then passed the light and turned facing the bright doorway.

Helios in such manner might appear to young Ion, facing in the black shade of Delphian myrtle-thicket, the twin hill-crests from which suddenly the sun would blind him. Only here, inappositely, the sun having blinded, there fell across his straining vision, just the utter sheer annihilating blackness that was simply the down-folding heavy curtain.

XVI

HEDYLUS SOUGHT BLINDLY for a few things, not heeding Hedyle. Hedyle, dear wraith, had shrunk; her proportion was all inadequate to the heroic world he moved in. Therefore obviously it behoved him to tend some kindness, to assume some manner, out of all proportion, tender.

"Yes. No, mother. I particularly hated it."

"You're tired. What were you up to?"

"The usual. Boredom and the pretentious dissertations of the new philosophers."

"Was the pavilion party really then a failure?"

"O, never, never, never. We drank heartily." He, inspired at this, declaimed with bright falsity,

> "Life is but vain,
> Unless I drink and drink again."

"You all read verses?"

"Um-um. That is to say, I emphatically."

"Which?"

"Some singular strange new ones."

"You have them ready?"

"Not yet quite." Again with bright falsity he shouted,

> "Strike, strike, O Loves,
> smite me and spare no ire."

It was as well he had met Sikeledes and Posidippus at the lower road-bend. The sudden moon had made a shining globe of each small white stone; the flowering quince had enchanted them all equally. The two were overcome with wine, and this other, this Hedylus with something different. Hedylus had emerged with exquisite pain from the cocoon of the old Hedylus; that latter they fraternally recognized. Hailed blithely. Embraced awkwardly, while a set Dionysiac mask (the face of Hedylus?), familiar to them yet somehow grown uncanny, transcendentalized by moon-magic, shouted their own verses.

> "Strike, strike, O Loves,
> smite me and spare no ire,
> O little silly mites;
> destroy with fire,
>
> giants of archery,
> and you shall be
> (attacking me alone,
> one against many)
> most famous, and O famously
> shall stand
> among the gods,
> imperviously grand."

It was Posidippus himself, the author of the brave lines, the less pacific but drunk now mainly with ecstatic loveliness of spring midnight, who reviled him. "Where were you?"

Hedylus had turned aside impertinence and in less time than it takes to tell, had in turn been informed of the success of the collected script, originally outlined for Douris.

"He wants the lot of us. He keeps repeating it. One cluster of Samian wild-flowers, wild-lily by anemone. He says the three of us will found a new academy." Posidippus was blatantly ironical; Sikeledes took the matter grandly. It seemed, in the grand manner, they were selected for divinity.

"We three. Not one. Not two. He wants the whole lot. *This* time its final. You *will* come, then?"

"But when?" from a detached Hedylus.

"The boat leaves any time at or after sunrise, depending on the sea-wind."

"Whose ever boat?"

"The simpleton. The small blighter."

"He's actually invited us?" Hedylus must hear the thing repeatedly.

"You, me, brother, him."

"For what dire and diabolic purpose?"

"Didn't you know? It's the talk, one learns, not only of wee Samos but of great Attica. We three are poets."

"Really? Since when?"

"Since chiefly, this gay evening."

Having re-dressed the anecdote for his mother's benefit to fit this new occasion, he added, "I shouldn't miss it, should I?"

"Ah, but the little man is horrible."

"I can't help that, can I? He thinks we're really poets."

"What right has he, with his cheap Alexandrian academy, to take all spring from Samos?" So she felt that way? Couldn't she have said that, just that "all spring from Samos" years and years ago? White ash; poor Hedyle! Spring had left Samos with the fall of a heavy curtain. Hedyle, grey phantom, was resting now in the false dawn and the late spluttering of lamps, in the same lion-footed chair, her lovely dinner-gown still wrapped about her; upon her frail arms, the unaccustomed bracelets.

"Mama, you never used," (they had had this out early this very evening; it seemed incredible; aeons of time had passed since), "to wear these things."

"Child," (she had said this too, aeons since), "they hide wrinkles."

He could, in his soul, say now, sing now, "you are my enemy, my mother; you are my enemy, my mother." He would, must, for that very flame of passionate discovery, therefore spare this wraith of grey impotence. He must spare, in order fully to escape from her. He must spare, in order fully to thwart now, Hedyle. For he was, wasn't he, no whit less violently and passionately severing his own soul from his own taut and flaming body? To leave Samos meant to leave, blatantly, crudely, this light of Delphic headlands, this stranger whom he worshipped.

"I know, mother, it's all very inopportune, very importunate. But leave I now must. You always (didn't you, while I was growing up and before we had that last authentic quarrel?) say when opportunity offered, I must be off to wider fields, to Alexandria or further still—" he stood tortured so to speak it, "to India."

"India?" She spoke as if she had never discussed with him in the old days, any of the Macedonian's dramatic provinces. "I never said I wanted you to leave me."

"No, mother." He found, surprisingly to himself, his soul intractable. He was broken more than she could ever guess at. He had for years suffered vicariously for Hedyle. His own suffering freed him now from spiritual incumbrance. He drew his armour, fire-tested breastplate across his spirit. Hiding with hardness this new fracture, this new thing, that had taken (in less time than it takes to tell it) place in him. This wound across his breast was tongue of pure flame; it relieved the pressure of his scalding forehead. Hard, separated at last, from his mother. She said, "is it that girl—Irene?"

Irene? He thought now of that Irene. Separated also from his consciousness. Irene was entombed in a rock-shrine, fittingly embalmed with wax-flower and with fragrance of white petal. Fittingly; herself might have chosen for herself that small headstone wreathed with salt-weed. Irene.

"O, Irene?" He caught himself in, lest over-carelessness betray him.

Hedyle flared at him, "you think yourself so clever? You think you've hidden this thing. You care, you all care for Irene."

"But, mother, she's a mere, blunt child."

"Nowadays men care for bluntness (if you can be termed in any sense—or those mighty fellow-poets—at all *men*), for wayward creatures, half-boys, lacking women's grace and virtue."

"*Vir*-tue?" He lingered ironic, wicked on the syllables. Hedyle was whipping out in bitterness, thwarted in anger, but ah, how futile, how far wide of the mark. *"Hedylus."* That strange affectation that even in her wildest anger did not leave her. That speech so fine, so musical, that differed, by just an overbreath from that of the native cultured islanders. Hedylus could not adequately define what it was in Hedyle's pronunciation, in the slight over-weighing of the syllables, that made her speaking reminiscent of another. That melted him, betrayed him, white flame of Delphic headlands. Behind a heavy forehead and a head bent forward and the firm, mighty upswing of muscular throat was the indubitable flash of gull-wings. Hedylus could not hate Hedyle. She was so pathetic, so impotent, so unilluminated.

"For years and years and years." His mother at least did not stoop to the cheap expedient of crying. It had been, he thought, far better for him (for her even) if only she could. He recognized a spirit sobbing, like some owl, blind at daybreak. To him day; to her dusk. They moved now absolutely and finally in separate orbits. "For years and years." They spoke different (though both Greek touched with

Athenian subtlety) tongues. Absolutely and forever, they were separated. "But didn't I too, do my part in striving? For years and years and years?" His gallantry, he now recognized, might have been his final ruin. He had never spoken to his mother but enthusiastically of these records. These tedious compilations and wearisome researches he had made for her and indirectly to keep Douris. Hadn't he been a spiritual as well as an intellectual tool of his mother? But adequately he was trained now, rewarded. He could, must make his way other-where, in some other land where he might forget that flaming Delphic headland.

"I don't want really," (could she know how truth spoke!), "to leave Samos."

"Why go, then?"

"Dear mother, haven't I told you twenty times this evening that if I go at all, I must go (depending on winds) almost immediately, possibly at daybreak?"

Hard pressed, she flung her last cast. "And you leave Irene?"

"No," he flared at her, "she's coming with us."

XVII

THIS TRULY WAS A NEW IDEA. It came suddenly, and through the curtains he had flung to, passionate in a moment, he noted above the mountain-crest that was simply their island Samos unsubmerged, a tenuous and exquisite break in a sky (faintest of rose through alabaster) of poignant silver.

"Dawn," he said, and knew Hedyle was, by that very inhuman symbol, adequately vanquished. "Could I stay here forever?"

She answered, "you've gone mad in a moment; over night. You were always thoughtful; obedient. Simple; almost undeveloped. Almost it seemed sometimes, subnormal in your felicitous devotion."

He answered, "mother, the smouldering silent and suppressed volcano is the one most dangerous."

She answered, "*you* a volcano? You, the most silent and sweetly guided; pasture spread with wild-flower."

Again he stared, astonished. "Couldn't you, mama, have said something like that, years ago?"

"Why say what was so adequately, in our subtlest moments, totally inexpressible?"

"Surely, you might just once (say three years ago) have said, 'child,' as you have a way of saying, 'I owe you everything.' "

"Things so deep as that one doesn't speak of." He regarded her closely, in the very cold that was the dawn. He
thought, "you too seared, scarred by something."

He said, "why bicker with it? It's better to go quickly. It
happened informally tonight—last night. At the—pavilion.
We were, as is usual (you know how it is with us,), shouting
verses. The little old creature singled out first of course,
Sikeledes." Hedylus thought now apart, a strange detachment, "yes, mother, his verse is beautiful." Standing with the
cold dawn spreading a mist of silver through the marble of
the open corridor, with Hedyle resplendent, like some cold
sea-goddess in her blue (odd metallic glitter that was her
latest iridescent import), he saw Hedyle as Thetis, himself
some lost child, no Achilles, and he whispered, simply with
that exquisite voiced breathing that was his straight Athenian
heritage,

> A flower of love is set beside
> a flower of loyalty; more fair
>
> than emerald set in gold
> or rare ebon by flawless ivory;
>
> yet gold proves less by the gem's light,
> not this by this; love set by love,
>
> Cleander, who is flower-of-love
> by flower-of-love, Eubiotos—

that's Sikeledes."

She answered, "his quality is repetitive, false. You might
do much better."

He turned, adequately disguised (he knew it) in that rare
daybreak. "No, mother, I've given all that up."

"Then you aren't going to be one of their hateful academic Alexandrian poets?"

"Ah," he answered, "I *am,* adequately."

XVIII

HE FOLLOWED SOME ALMOST CLAIRVOYANT VISION, leaving Hedyle in that silver streak of unflattering and in human dawn, drawn, singularly withered. Blue and passionate lily, hadn't she had her whim, her will, through all these—centuries, he was about to mutter. It seemed centuries since he had last faced her in full simplicity, a field (as she expressed it) spread with wild-flower. His naiveté had been, in one straight moment, shattered. In one second; so things so high-purposed, flawless things of the intellect, must happen. How long ago was it that he had stood by the cavern where he had laid a forehead as against some mighty altar? Some half-day? Some half-million aeons? Now he recognized in the first dawn, the same scent of cliff-flower; he recalled the upflung pearl of broken berries...

Like some clairvoyant, he knew just where he'd find Irene. Clairvoyance though, was hardly necessary to the occasion. Didn't she always slip her nets at dawn across the low shoals? Didn't she boast, her wayward child pathetic little boast, that she had the best eyes for shellfish, crayfish, mussels, wrasse in all the island? Well, anyhow, he'd chance it. Bustle and preparation of the wharf-hands; curtains drawn before the wealthy villas; clump and heady cluster of Greek lilies against the upflung plinth of the new, sophisticated Artemis of the headlands; small shrines in the poorer quarters, where bundles of faded saffron lay, offering to god of fertility; down the twisting poorer streets where, even through the sordid low doorways and past the rubble of old boats, of fresh lumber for the fitting-out of hulks, of all the rope and sail-cloth and scattering of débris, the fragrance of the quince-flower followed him; growing in low earth-pots were heavy clusters—again of the Greek lily; and turning by the Priapus of the Fishers with its offerings (old nets, draggled by weather, gross carved emblem, gifts of simple-minded fisher, piously offered to the god whose soul despises nothing), he met Irene.

"Hedylus, alert at daybreak?" she jeered; always she had that manner with her.

He said, "yes, for some unaccountable reason. This old blue-nose (you made such fun of) turns out to be the most flagrant of philosophers. He's founding an academy. But you know this. Or has founded one in Alexandria."

She pulled her dripping salt nets across bared legs and, where a great gash dripped scarlet, a flat tunny fish squirmed and flattened, beat against the blue of her skirt that dragged wet and heavy at the girdle of knotted hemp ends. Her small, childlike face was set in too heavy a frame of beautifully carved bone. The heavy bone beneath the boylike structure of the forehead seemed to draw too fine the wax-like texture of the white skin. Across heavy framework of Spartan bone and fibre was laid, as an unfitting garment, the most exquisite of rose-shell and white flesh. The hands held, taming the wriggling object. The fish turned, flapped; the heavy flap-flap, of his flat body was reminiscent of the wave he leapt from. Across the dark loose sleeve, salt (dried some days past) made white pattern as of frost-flower.

"And Hedylus?" A voice, unlike Hedyle's spoke short syllables. Hedylus did not fear overwhelming, inordinate beauty when he faced Irene.

"Hedylus," he answered briefly, "sails with blue-nose."

"Not that object?"

"Why not, sweet Irene?"

Strange, contradictory, enormous tears betrayed Irene, though she made no movement forward, nor changed her wide expression.

"Irene crying?"

"This awful smell of salt fish."

"Yes" he answered, "come with me back to village Samos, up-stairs, again. We'll meet the others. Irene shall wave farewell, blithely from the headland."

HE FELT SINGULARLY, a dank indrawing as if his very intestines were drawn, by some unaccountable nerve-action, inward, to scrape against a hollow left by some hours' fasting and this devastating fracture with his mother. A tight, almost perceptibly outlined oval was his empty inside, as if some leather bag, empty and unpalatable, had been substituted and now empty, grazed his long, perceptibly outlined backbone. Considering this on the familiar steps above the sordid thatched row of fishers' huts, he leaned against the wall at the stairs' narrow turning; a nausea assailed him. He seemed, by some unaccountable blunder, to have lost his foothold, to be slipping, though he realized he stood static, with firm feet on the broad wet stairway. Lilies innumerable from above the grey stones of the fishers' village, flung intolerable, heady fragrance. Above the wall, lilies of glazed translucent whiteness. Lilies of some unparalleled and unaccountable growth; stark, Greek, intractable.

He said, "Irene." Noticed a firm, heavy rose and white, coral and pearl-shell, small weight of heavy hand (Irene's) upon the stained linen of yesterday's somewhat too festive tunic. Upon the drawn thread of his bright sleeve he noticed (while against his spine something heaved and sank) a small child-hand that held power, force, altogether demigod-like. His shoulders scraped the dank wall. He felt the thin blades, pushed them to some physical reality of torture, so that he might fully and adequately realize his material entity, his sheer physical condition.

"Last night. Don't tell Hedyle—"

She said, "when do I ever see or speak to Hedyle, save in most formal manner? And should I ever anyway, speak to her of—you?"

He said, parenthetically, foregoing for the moment straight confession, "why, Irene, shouldn't you ever speak to her of Hedylus?"

She answered, "Hedyle doesn't know at all our Hedylus." Her voice was positive, firm in outline. Its syllables were hard, somewhat unfamiliar, somewhat foreign. Her very pronouncement of his name brought him to his senses.

He announced starkly in a trance-like manner, "I must say simply, yesterday while I re-read some wild informal metres (I will leave them below the cliff path) while you others were elaborating verses upstairs, I met—a creature."

"One of the new delegation from Macedon, going to India?"

"I suppose so. Anyhow, he said I must go with him."

"You just said you were going with old blue-nose to (wasn't it?) Alexandria?" For the first time she noticed his face drained of its colour and his clenched teeth. Now letting go, shivering, his teeth began to chatter.

"Jibbering," he said, "you see, I'm jibbering."

She stood a step below him and dropped her net which slid slowly two steps downward, heaved with the struggle of the still vibrant monster and then lay heavily static. She propped, fisher-like, her elbows and so held him.

"Who was it that you saw, then?"

He answered, his thin arm in its bright and somewhat too festive tunic, lax, bodiless across her sturdy rough-clad and salt-wetted shoulder, "Helios."

Irene spoke, decisive, domineering. "Come, Hedylus," shaking him a little. "You say you leave with Sikeledes and with Posidippus for Alexandria. I noted when I passed the wharf, preparation for some boat's departure. Listen. Come just so far as the wharf. They have large space of cabins for the Alexandrians. You'll find a couch, some bedding, wool and fleeces. You'll rest there, Hedylus."

She shook, with her vibrant strength the lax and weary figure, "speak. You've gone, got somewhat lost. Where are you?"

He answered, "Irene; I'm standing with you on the steps of Thanksgiving-for-the-full-nets, on the turn out of the fishing-village. Behind us are the thatched huts. Above us, if we ever get there, is the new sophisticated and to me, somewhat too realistic Artemis of Headlands. Beyond, is the narrow path that twists through dwarf cytisus and the wild-myrtle. The myrtle is not flowering but the wax-flower is dropping below in the secret cavern; white berries unflung like scattered seed-pearl."

She said, "yes, Hedylus," drawing him toward the upper stairway, "come to the boat. I'm coming with you. I'm coming...staying with you. Tell me about your work and—Helios."

XIX

HEDYLE LIFTED THE OUTER WRAP she had a moment since flung upon the low couch. She drew it close about her and wandered toward the curtains. No. Let them stay drawn. Lyda had put out the fading lamps. She was quite right. It was time one got some sleep now. The boat would or would not sail, depending on the weather. It was drawn. Unflattering to wrinkles. One never knew who might or who might not be at the landing.

She let the wrap slip from her shoulders and turned toward the dressing-table. After all, why go out? but then, after all, why not? She lifted the polished mirror. A face regarded her in blotting shadows. It was the face of Hedyle the Athenian. It had that look, godlike tranquility, that comes to some, at overwhelming odds with destiny. The somewhat flagrant earrings did not minimize at this moment its curious spirituality.

"Douris has understood me."

She said, "Douris has understood me" to the mirror and wondered why she said it. She had consistently maintained that Douris always bored her. "I must go to Douris. Now. Tell him about the boat. His loss of Hedylus. After all, it's *his* loss of Hedylus." She put down the polished mirror. It seemed to her in a moment that she was unaccountably

117

drawn to Douris. Hadn't he authentically protected her boy? Shielded him?

"What had I to give Douris in exchange for what he gave me? I chattered nobly. I chattered on and on and could have gone on chattering until doomsday. The Furies tonight (last night) walked on my grave. Didn't I simply feel it? I knew something was about to happen. It was as if a heavy foot had been planted on our Samos. Samos is a small place, a sort of stepping-stone from Europe on to...Asia...or Alexandria. It has no part in the great scheme of matters. Samos is a stepping-stone and tonight (last night?) it seemed some step trod heavily on Samos. The whole place tottered."

She drew off the over-garment and ran her hand along it. "This thing by lamplight was like light on water. It takes a heavier quality without lights." She moved half-instinctively to call again for lamps. "I can't face this day."

She piled a handful of odd ornaments on her low dressing-table and decided not to get fresh lamps. A great crack from the carelessly drawn curtain made a clear wedge of dramatic light across the dark rug; square of solid metal on the red cloth. The rich cloth seemed to turn under her very eyes into some field of thick-set violets or rich winter-flowering cyclamen. "Hedylus loved wild-flowers. Of course I've been right. There could be no two ways about it. If I had succumbed to his mere charm, charmed him as I could have done with myth and poetry, I could have kept him. I could have kept the child by wounding him, blunting his fervid intellect. I saw from the first he had it." For a moment Hedyle forgot to be Athenian. "You can't love a boy and bring it up a sword...a solid weapon...when he hasn't got a father."

The word brought something to her eyes. "I'm not crying. I did everything I could do. I had to put a sword in his hand so that he could fight, so that when necessary he could fight me. I knew the moment would come, if he were important, when he would do it. Superficially, all the time, I resisted Hedylus. Under my armour, my resistance, my love waited like a field of mountain wild-flowers waiting for protective ice to melt and cherish it like warm rain. I can't see, couldn't ever see my way to tell it. To tell the child I loved him would have reduced my staid determination to another formula. It would have been not Athené with young Ion or Erechtheus, bringing him to power and strength in order to serve Athens...but some later Cyprian. The Cyprian was shielded...one after another. Ares. She had one after another god to serve her. I had only myself to serve myself. Only Hedyle to serve Athens.

"Strictly speaking, I knew the gods had duped me. I didn't accept that predicament fully till this moment..." Hedyle spoke with no resentment. She ran her thin dynamic claw-like fingers over the garment she had slipped off her shoulders. The clasp that had formalized its folds lay glittering gold and amber where she dropped it. The garment had fallen simply when she undid the buckle at the shoulder. The gem on the shoulder-clasp had held her attention momentarily as she placed it by the bracelets and ear-rings on the table. Then she had stooped and lifted the cloth like some wood-nymph conjuring water. The garment was conjured out of the tufts (so to speak) of the carpetlike jet of water from a field edging some dark-bushed forest. The shadows were dark, a forest confronting her. The light made solid wedge across the carpet. Herself standing in her simple undergarment was some nymph simply. "I sometimes think I've forgotten what it's all like—playing, I mean, as I used to do with Clio. I never played with my own child. He was so terrible...a stark responsibility."

The garment flowed from her fingers. She recognized a mood she had thought long since suppressed out of consciousness. "It was like this with Clio. Clio my sister, not the mistress of Apollo. Clio and I used to run water through our fingers." The garment shimmered as she held it. "After all, I'm Hedyle of Athens."

She said, "I'm Hedyle of Athens," but she was no such considerable person. She was a child that had been housed a long time, dazed before sudden freedom. The curtain at her back widened the strip of light across the carpet. The carpet certainly was cyclamen. She noted the silver had sudden edge of rayed fire. Gold. "The sun is getting higher. Is that you, Lyda?"

The voice answered her in courteous Greek. "Forgive me this intrusion."

Hedyle turned with her erratic gesture, the one-two that she had been taught as a child marks the aristocratic turn of heels at proffered greeting. Not slithering with the feet on the floor. (Lyda used to say, "don't slither. Be autocratic, children.") She made such a set turn as children make before their formal elders. She was revealed for what she always had been, quaintly even as a small child. Greek simply. Things that from the first she had been disciplined to. To which she had disciplined her son. The gesture brought her back to herself, not this self, something remote with Clio. She thought vaguely, "I don't know what it is. Athens seems nearer." She was still fingering the stuff, veiling the light before her. "Someone's been sent by Douris to tell me that the boat's left."

The voice inquired of Hedyle in familiar Greek if she was that simply. It said "Hedyle," as if there could be another in Laconia or Corinth or some island of the Cyclades, "the Athenian?" Hedyle was that in Samos. She did not have to start backward at that rare inflection. "The Athenian." It was the way he said it. Hedyle knew the garment would not hide her. She held it nevertheless persistently before her as if her mind were bent, concentrated solely on this one thing. She examined the fibre critically as if for some suspected break or flaw in the fine texture. . .for through its iridescent folds she saw a head bent forward. The heavy and commanding beauty of a firm chin. The shoulders of the deity of Delphi. She saw God simply.

"Is that Demion of Olympia?"

He said, "they called me that sometimes."

She said, watching him through the stained stuff, "I've had many visions, dreams, presentiments. This thing is yourself simply."

He said, "Hedyle of Athens, I have never left you."

She said, "I know that. You spoiled everything."

Her manner as she dropped the garment, facing him, was suddenly commonplace, unethereal, unspiritual, remotely un-Athenian. Her mood, her manner had degenerated with the going of her rival. A brain had glowed steadily beside her, a sword had pointed constantly at her. Her own son had been her standard, her threat, her constant heart-ache. She was glad, with some curious sloughing-off of spirit, now he had gone.

"I've lost Hedylus."

Her head felt as if some heavy helmet had been lifted from it. Some hand had removed a helmet with valiantly uplifted bright crest, from a torn forehead. Hedyle felt a strip as of searing metal where the rim was. Lately a rim had bound her forehead, only a few hours lately. Only a few hours since, she had heard verses, criticized words, faulty metres. How could such things matter? It seemed that metres, words alike, had been removed with that cruel metal.

"Hedylus has left Samos." She spoke as one in a trance; the words meant nothing. She was glad he had left. She wondered why tears inconsistently deterred her from seeing this thing opposite. A stained bright veil had blinded her, now grey tears. She saw blindly (as one half blind) a grey

form outlined in light that was slurred over as with rain-
drops. The sun glowed in fitful sparks like sparks thrown
from metal. Metal was blue. Could be blue sometimes. That
serpent bracelet. "I don't see anything." She was still standing. Still facing blinding dawn-light, veiled as it happened in
this dim mist. "I can't understand it." She was glad Hedylus
had left Samos. Why was she crying? She was happy simply.
Something had been lifted from her tired head. "I don't think
I've been myself for ten years."

She turned with the aristocratic click of sandals, then
said destructively, with a gamin gesture, "it's too bad I
washed the kohl off. I always do before I start undressing."
She was speaking with deliberated unrefinement, un-
Athenian. She seemed to have been walking for all these
years in a false light, mouthing as behind a mask from some
elevated height toward a grinning amphitheatre of unfriendly
people. Or friendly. Did it matter? Stage-set simply. She
seemed to have been revolving in a false light, thinking in a
false area of consciousness. "I should have ruined the boy's
mind if I had told him of you."

He said, "what was there to tell, Hedyle?"

She said, "everything. Papa had taught Clio and me the
fantasies of numbers. We grew up in strange surroundings.
Papa was so fantastic. But if it hadn't been for his silly Attic
sternness, I'd have succumbed to you."

He bowed and she moved forward, indicating the couch
placed sideways by the doorway. He sat, his heavy and commanding beauty half-shadowed by the curtain.

She said, "Demion, why have I always loved you? How
has that remained in a world of constant wreckage, flowers
being broken, frost smiting knife-wise, evil marring beauty?
How have you stayed—Demion?"

He said, "in the same way that you have stayed
—Hedyle. I didn't need to come back to demonstrate that to

you. To Hedyle the Athenian, logical and comprehending."

She said, "why did you come back? Is it to ensnare Hedylus?"

He said, "one doesn't snare a wild bird with the starlight."

She said, "one does. *You* do. One does snare souls with beauty."

He said, "I didn't quite snare Hedyle."

She said, "is that what (after ten years) you've come back to tell me?"

He said, "a thing so obvious as that needs no crude ornament of awkward word-stuff."

The slight inflection of over-civilization she recognized almost as a mockery of her own speech. *Things so near, deep as that one doesn't speak of.* She had said that lately. *Things inexpressible*—where had she last so spoken?

It was in this room. Here recently. It was true that time was a wily being, running in and out of one's fingers like cold water. She flung the garment on the floor. She watched it, half-thinking it would sink down, be drawn into the glowing carpet like blue water into flower-tufts. The garment lay resplendent in that sunlight. She stooped and shook it with ironic gesture. "Shall I re-dress in last night's dinner garment? Or does one find other things for visitors at this hour?" Her words were petulant. She was tired. Demion, if he were Demion, might have chosen some more opportune time for his appearance. He always was dramatic. But this was too consistent.

"I've thought of you every hour for some ten years."

"It's longer than that."

"After ten years, I just left off counting. I said, in ten years maybe; ten years seemed a complete cycle. At first, I said three years. I was certain you'd re-emerge after three years; then five years; then the mysterious infallible seven.

Seven years of infallible waiting didn't bring you. I was tired of waiting. Waiting that is, with fervid spiritual integrity. Since, I have lived with Douris. Seven years. Then ten years. And then I left off counting."

The mirror lay where she had left it, scanning her perfect features last (was it only last?) night. The disc of the mirror glowed cold and certain. It was a certain, touchable thing. Silver. A polished metal that showed one's face alive, clear like a figure carved static on some great intaglio. Hedyle felt for the handle of the familiar object and, lifting it, let drop again the mysterious blue and iridescent shimmer of the spun cloth. Her incredibly slender index again sought out familiar marking. This line is this. This is the head of the vine-god wreathed in grape-leaf and this is the band of Satyrs. The silver mirror gave her new certainty. Demion was waiting by her. The silver mirror gave her a clue to go by. It was something symbolic, something to hold on to, like the moon giving reason and formula to the goddess Delia. Delia was the sister of the Delphian. Who was still there.

"I mean the boy. I never meant to have him. Clarix, my first lover, had betrayed me. It was all due to papa. He was so remote. There was no competing with him. No one ever taught us. The thing was a shock. Had nothing to do with formula, with numbers, with the why and the why, not even with philosophic dissertations of my uncle from Cyrene. Papa was so fantastic. And Clio wasn't well that year. Clarix shocked me, and with a turn, I ran straight to the arms of . . . I can't even name him. There was Clarix and this other. It seemed impossible. I lay on a rock outside Sunium, where we stayed with Lyda. Papa was so fantastic. There were, he had assured us, no gods. There was a fiery pain at the back of my head and I had been taught that pure reason was the only goodness. Goodness. Goddess. There were others, I was certain. There was the Cytherean. I said, I will know. I needn't

have this infant. I'll close my eyes, and if...
if...something...happens, then I'll have it."

Hedyle spoke to the back of the polished mirror. She
held on to it. It gave her definition. Symbolism. It was symbolic like the bracelet with the serpent biting its own tail.

"I closed my eyes and prayed (as papa had told us was all
wrong) to...to any god that was there. I said to myself,
when I opened my eyes if there is a sign, I'll have it. I'll have
this child of...even then I couldn't name him. There was a
curious pain at the back of my head. It might have been the
sunlight. I opened my eyes expecting to see Aphrodite rising
from the shining water. My first thought was of relief. No
god had answered. Papa *was* right."

Hedyle put aside the mirror. It had given her what she
wanted. A sense of continuity, of her own person. I am
Hedyle of Athens. This is my mirror, my room, my dressing-
chest, my inlaid lapis-box. I am Hedyle of Athens. The mirror made her see Hedyle of Athens as a projection, yet herself
certainly. Hedyle. Hedyle.

She said, "Hedyle" again and then said, "Hedylus. The
reason that I had him was the simplest. The most illiterate.
After the first cynical certainty that papa was right and no
foam and froth and white apparition crowned with divine
sweet rose-leaf had re-emerged from the water about
Sunium, or ever would do to any man's entreaty, I had the
shock. I had said, 'if I have a sign, I will have Hedylus.' A
small creature was staring where no creature had stared. It
was only a little grass-snake. It was the most ordinary of tiny
reptiles. It stared straight at me. It must have been staring, it
gave that odd appearance, for a long time. It must have been
there while I searched the livid water for the rare sign, the apparition rising to reclaim me, servant of Love, Hedyle for
Cyprus. The Cyprian didn't want Hedyle, at that moment.
There was a small snake, but I knew as one does know that it

wasn't any snake out of ordinary time, out of ordinary dimension, yet it *was* all the time (this really was the miracle) a real entity, a real being, one that anyone might see. Perhaps not *anyone*, but 'Clio' I remember saying, 'see if you see anything.' As a matter of fact, I still half-left the oracle to Clio. If Clio had said, 'I see the grey rocks, the tufts of the thyme,' this or this or this, describing as she always did, everything precisely, grass-blades and the exact forms of them, fringes under rock, spikes against sky, I should have discountenanced the thing as vision. I called her, said 'come, Clio.' I laughed and said, 'look. There is a sign straight from divinity. Do you see something?' Clio said 'there is a green snake and I hate reptiles.' She slid off the rock-side and that was all. But it *was* there. Because the answer came so irrevocably, yet so casually, I believed there were gods. This was the signet of the god of Delphi. The sun was hot as ever any sun could be. I lay open to his glamour on that rock. This child, I said, won't be the child of Clarix or of the other lover. I would see to it. I said, 'I'll have the child because of that snake but it will be the sun's child.'

"I must have been mad . . . O, the whole thing was a fantasy. I was so ill. Yet everything somehow helped me. Everything came right. Poor papa didn't even know about it. That winter the plague took him. Clio was married. There was nothing for me. I waited, believing god would emerge, shield me. There is such a thing as waiting too long. When the boy was a year old, I found you."

Her head was in her hands. The high suspense of her clear vision had unnerved her. "I never was so tired as this. Possibly that one night . . . in Athens."

She flung back her head expecting to face an empty space of curtain. She had talked this way to herself often. She had talked this out to herself, in such simple words that no one could mistake them. She had formed this habit of simple thought in regard to Hedylus, almost from the first; for almost from the first she had thought that she must tell him. She considered it her great intellectual triumph that she had not. But the speech (the simple dramatic wording of it) remained fixed in her memory so that at a moment, with the falling of a shadow in clear sunlight, with the unexpected scutter of wild-feet or bird-wing outside her window, she could form words, make words suit the inexpressible. Outline her formula, her code, the reason for her faith and the reassurance of her hard-won absolution.

She had made this speech so often to a shadow. She flung back her head, not thinking to see Demion.

XX

"DEMION OF OLYMPIA, you are there. Demion. Daemon or Demon. I knew you were *God.* I waited for some sign from you (from God) after I had Hedylus. Then, I gave that up. All I could do was to leave the child with Lyda. Then there was space of thinking. Thought came back after those months of physical upheaval, isolation and discomfort. I thought clearly.

"I said I was duped. I had asked for a sign when, my mind in its first trap, in the first springing of the trap, I was off-guard. I had walked blindly down and down into the recesses of the trap, for my mind, off-guard, had perceived an apparition. Not a vision, a dream, something translatable in simple numbers or thought, but the absolutely certain transmutation of spirit into matter. Argument couldn't have convinced me that that little reptile was just any little reptile crawled out one day (any day) in spring, to sun his green and blue and emerald scales on hot rocks. He was and wasn't to be explained away just as Demion, when he appeared, might have been (was, to any human understanding) Demion of Olympia, of exact antecedent, of exotic and slightly erratic habits.

"O, Demion, he travels, he comes and goes, he never lets us know his whereabouts. *You* might all the time have been regarding me out of the husk of the thing called Demion. Demion the translatable man, might have himself been in India, in the Hesperides, in Scythia. Demion travelled. Demion, as the world knew him, might have been dead even. There was that certainty when I faced you in the lily-corridor of Demetrius, that I was seeing double.

"I saw Demion of Olympia as the world must see him, as the casual greeting Demetrius gave you in passing assured me existed in the world's eyes. Demion comes and goes. Having accepted the fact that you were some apparition allied in consciousness to the small serpent of Hedylus' pre-birth, I couldn't trap you. There was no use. I could ask about Demion, but, having accepted the fact of your duality, I had to say to myself, if he is Delphic to that extent, he could easily *assume* the manner, the habit, the appearance of another, might *borrow* so to speak, the appearance of Demion for the occasion. God, the god you were or served exactly, was too subtle to appear, a flaming star, with bow and searing arrows. The day of such apparition had long passed. God to be recognizable must take, as a cloak, the habiliment of a mortal.

"Thought that would entrap you, would nullify you. For if I said yes, yes, yes, this is Demion, a traveller, a man of parts, master of military science, an autocrat and savant, then I should lose the god. I couldn't do that. If I had said, this is a god, an adept at apparition, then I must lose the so perfect materialization of...just what I wanted. A man, someone understanding me and Athens.

"A flame was in your eyes. You might have been god or man. Both claimed me. How then, could I fail either? I didn't lose my sense of my position, my dignity, even though I was guest in that hateful house, as I smiled back at you. I knew that it was some test of spirit, of autocratic greatness, of (in a word) equality. If I had given away, screamed like

Cassandra, it wouldn't have been remarkable. I had had the illness after Hedylus, and papa had been swept off by the plague, and such as couldn't any more endure me for my wraith-beauty (like Demetrius) tolerated me for that famous, much (then) exploited wit (may God forgive me) I was noted for. Yet neither wit nor semblance of wraith-beauty helped me, facing Demion of Olympia. Yet it *did* help. Both helped. You weren't (were you?), I consoled myself, likely to waste so exquisite a gesture on just—no-one.

"Hedyle of Athens had proved autocracy. Hedyle of Athens, having proved it, for an illiterate moment had let go autocracy; it was—well, awkward having the child Hedylus. Hedylus of Athens had been, in a word, my test, and I dare say everyone has just some such awkward moment. Facing the path direct between intellectual greatness and something...other. Delphi was full of illiterate beggars, thieves, twisters of the oracle. It was in ill-repute, those years in Athens. So, for the matter of that, wasn't every one of our Greek oracles? We were a dusty, tired people. War and war and war. Papa was so fantastic. In the face of pure proven fact, he would insist that numbers were imperishable. Clio and I were fantastically reared. When I decided I couldn't be your mistress, I went back at the last, at least intellectually, to papa."

The words, the childish phrasing of the sentences, sustained her. It was not a witty woman that was speaking but a tired one. "I wouldn't accept that invitation to travel on to India. I know just that much. I had seen God in a flash. I knew you looked out of a borrowed body. Demetrius had been glad to shelter me for a time and would have been glad permanently to house me...Demetrius. You saved me from that fate, anyhow. It was as if you had turned a river from its course at a moment of suspense, arrested it for an imperceptible fraction of second, before it lost its identity in low-lying marshes. Demetrius' assembly . . . a sluggish river. It is hard to think of Hedyle, Athenian autocrat and intellectual, as a sluggish river. At the moment—I was that.

"You said to me, 'let me have Hedylus.'

"Hedylus hadn't been asked for nor inquired about by either Clarix or that other. You were the first man, just human-shouldered mortal, who had asked tenderly of my child. O, I was very silly. I was so weak, so stricken by the plague, Demion, that I made you an immortal. Not for anything even of eyes shining like a lizard's; not for the unescapable beauty of your body; not for the bearing that acclaimed your kingship; but because at a moment when my soul was sluggish and Demetrius offered me rest and loss of personal identity (the ache of weary thinking), you acclaimed me.

"You saw Hedyle of Athens not as Hedyle the intellectual but as indubitably a woman. You saw the thing in me that had been nearly blighted. You saw me as a lover. I was so ill, so childish, so surprised that I made a god of you. Forgive me, Demion of Olympia."

XXI

"I SAY FORGIVE ME, and why do I say that? The lilies that lined the corridor of Demetrius that night were so many tongues to leer and mouth at me and have been. I cherish such lilies daytime, in my terraces. At night, they reward my assiduous care by returning to my inner room for converse. Nights they stare at me, glare somewhat, occasionally revile me.

"A god wanted Hedyle of Athens (if he was God), and Hedyle of Athens (if there ever was an Athens) was so besotted with her own decrepitude that she spurned him.

"Many times, cool and impartial in the throne-room of this Douris, I might have been Cassandra. The more cold and remote they thought me, the more a voice screamed (but adequately suppressed) within me. Cassandra saw God openly and spurned him. So Hedyle of Athens. For if you were, as seemed most credible, some materialized divinity, it seemed also credible that you might want a . . . lover. The gods themselves grow weary being lonely. I found that out . . . Yet if I had screamed wildly, what was there? Cassandra was a forsaken creature, moreover finally an outcast.

"No. I wasn't thus forsaken. No one could prove my mind's infirmity, and I had my—dignity, a useless attribute and cherished as acidly (it sometimes seemed to me) as ugly virgins' never-tempted virtue. What is dignity or virginity? Attributes that one doesn't mark till they're lost simply. I clung ridiculously to mine. Dignity as ridiculous as an ugly woman's virtue. Yet I kept it. If Cassandra had loved madly, how differently then Hedyle! I must retain my sanity, prove sane to love you. Cold helmet of light might lie across my forehead, would always after some flaming midnight torn with torture. Peace came always with the morning. I would prove fit lover for you by retaining sanity, retaining immortality.

"So the boy should do. I wasn't going to blind his mind with fables. If his father were a god, you simply, resplendent, making yourself appear to me one day at holy Sunium, then it were better, if he shouldn't know it. If I were duped, as seemed most possible, then he should not (by actual reasoning) be fooled in the same manner. If I had attained a glamorous victory of the mind over the mere physical defilement of child-bearing, then how could he share it with me? If I had been fooled, then my own fate should warn him. Not openly, you understand, my Demion (Daemon or Demon), but in a thousand subtle insinuating manners. Ways. Manners. The child was no ordinary creature.

"The turn came in the lily-corridor of Demetrius. I simply saw you and didn't scream about it. It was something to have seen you, a test simply. And if I did in some odd way repudiate divinity for a lover, by that same repudiation, I retained you. Weren't women, so importunate as to let God love them, always later tacitly abandoned? Ariadne? Creusa? Not to name twenty others. Or appositely, like Cassandra, driven to hysteria? I wanted something other for divinity. I made the famous gesture: I did and didn't give way to your beauty.

"You must have been pleased, were, I saw it, with my gesture. Pleased not with the thing I had done, but with its originality; it differed so from any other mortal's feeble tactics. Your eyes were white in that corridor. I know them perfectly. They gleam at me in the darkness like a cat's eyes, phosphorescent. You have never left me. As a god, you never left me. As a mortal, it was obvious, you were the perfect lover. Antidote to Clarix and...that other. You offered everything that I never had been offered, strength with beauty simply. What man can give it to a high-bred woman? You were the calm, the antidote, to all my suffering.

"Paeon came when I had seemed past healing. It was as if spring had twice risen, twice to be driven back by hail-stones, and had a third time mounted (as inevitably as the jonquil) from the shadows. Persephone twice risen and twice defeated was in my face, I know, as I looked at you. I was so much a projection of myself even then, that I could regard myself as in a mirror, wonder really that no one had before spoken so exquisitely. It seemed odd that I should have escaped, in spite of my obvious outward indifference, from tenderness. Hedyle of Athens. Hedylus of Athens. When you asked me of my small son, I was a human being and was surprised that no one else had so asked.

"I was, they said it, a work of art, and I was, they saw it, unfortunate in my peculiar physical predicament. Whom could I tell? Not Clio. Papa was dead and anyhow he had seriously taught me to believe the Delphic godhead was illiterate. Necromancy was a word held over me in childhood. Delphic mantic illiteracy. I had asked for a sign. Helios, the god of signs, the mantic deity, had shown me...a small serpent not much larger that a largish lizard. Just that one day at Sunium.

"I didn't at first entirely realize what you were. I was broken by that prevision of mortality. Men could care, did care even for Hedyle, who had twice risen to flower, who had twice been driven back into the shadows. I felt I was doomed for loving. I loved you so, so ardently adored you that I feared to lose you. O, it went round and round like that tiny green-white serpent biting it's own tail."

Hedyle stepped toward the dressing-table. "This bracelet. I wore it because of that small reptile. It came from a coffin, from a girl from Egypt.

"You asked me to go to Egypt. To go to India. Demetrius' corridor spun round and round at your words. The lily-vestibule and the lily-corridor were that simply. I was imprisoned in a great flower and your words were bees (O your voice) droning their numbing message. There was (those bee-notes intoned) absolute beauty, love for Hedyle. I was so numb with your astute beauty that I stared at you, and you knew though I did not say it that I could not, no, *would* not go with you to India.

"The corridor was a whirl and then the house stood static. I recalled my surprise that a room could stand so quiet, planted square on rock. A room on rock. Demetrius' house was over-painted, over-crowded with celebrity. Coming and going. But the wrong sort. With Demetrius, I could have sunk identity. I loved Athens, could have sunk identity in Athens. Douris was different. Douris had (later) just that gesture of firm shoulders. He captured me through Hedylus. Athens was no place for Hedylus, the child of Hedyle the Athenian.

"Hedylus. Hedyle. We were too close, a single sort of being. For that reason, I spared him this thing, this part of me the child could never guess at. My share in immortality...or my share in illiteracy.

"You sit stolid there in daylight, Demion of Olympia, but I don't altogether, even now, accept you."

Her intellectual passion had not so far outdone her that she forgot that she was tired, must look ill, wizened a little and out-done. Hedyle thought of herself always in terms of herself and she saw herself facing Demion of Olympia, clearly. She saw herself as a tired woman, grown ill and worn with waiting.

"I waited too long for you."

Hedyle walked resolutely to the doorway. She flung wide the curtain and was sustained almost as by a miracle. For the moment at least, the dawn was over-shadowed and the sky itself seemed a gentle curtain to enfold her. She hadn't cared for wrinkles, wished he would look. If he were that Demion of Olympia and no erratic deity, he would see how she had faded.

"I am a blue lily, flung," she said, "at dawn upon a dust-heap." Her determination this time to see clearly, now sustained her. "I am Hedyle of Athens drained of sap, of life, and of vitality." If he were a crude lover, returned after these years to view the toll of conquest, then let him see her clearly. "I loved you so much that I stayed with Douris because he had shoulders like you. I clung speechless at night to iron shoulders and recalled a rock that had faced me with Demetrius. Demetrius was the lowest, the thing that would have freed me, lost me my identity and my soul with it. Demion was something out of intellectual calculation and I feared like Cassandra, I should go mad with thinking. Rush headlong, pronouncing to a sceptic universe that I had seen God. People don't any more care if one does see God. God remains mysterious; they must worship him in temples, pile up formula, confuse him with their ethic. God remains, perhaps always has, a little outside human consciousness. You plunged in, more humanly than any man could. If you had stood beside me in flaming sandals the night that I had Hedylus, I should have been assured but not comforted.

"You waited until I was utterly forsaken. Then came to me, not as a shining apparition but as a mere man. God to attain his immortality does that. He attains humanity. But what use? To whom could I tell this? I have been a blind Cassandra smitten with my secret. I have been Clytie not daring to follow the sunrise to his setting. I have been each separate and individual member of the Pierian circle without the sun-god to sustain my faith in my own singing. I have lived like the swan hiding his song in secret."

Hedyle replaced the serpent-bracelet on her fore-arm. "No. Not utterly in secret. This for example. I pretended you had sent it."

XXII

"CLIMAX AND ANTICLIMAX. That is what life is. Things slide over things. I mean, it was like the Acropolis that day you left me. It seemed as if a perfect image of the Acropolis had been slipped across the old one, as if a thing of transparent ice, crystal, had been slipped over the old stone. The stones of the Acropolis had seemed dead things, simply stones cut and laid there. Sometimes when the sun was near the horizon, the hills (you know them) became a solid cup of colour. A flower. One heart of one anemone. The violet-crowned. The violet-weaving. The Muses of Apollo. O, Hedyle of Athens with scepticism for a father saw the Acropolis set upon the Acropolis, or at least that is the only possible way to explain it. So with these things. There comes a moment when life seems overlaid with immortality as a flower with pure dew; like a flower-bud sustained beneath water, held and nourished. So this super-life seems to descend sometimes, to lie across one's whole vision. It was so with Hedylus . . ."she had come back to the beginning, a serpent biting its own tail.

"He didn't as a child matter so very much. He mattered as an actual manifestation of an act of faith. I had him, had faith to have him because a serpent stared at me steadily in sunlight. Did I argue myself into hysteria? Did I make up the fact of your identity with beauty? Maybe. But the very fact of my faith that could so far plunge forward into the infinite, held me like some jewel weighing a dead body to earth.

"The body this came from," she lifted her arm, ringed with the serpent-bracelet, "was weighed down with ornament. So Hedyle. My belief in your identity with beauty has held me earth-bound. My body but for that would have been dissolved, rotted into the baser elements. I have been a corpse wrapped like that Egyptian's, in my own faith. I lived and in living preserved dynamic power enough to convince an ordinary mortal (this Douris) that I too was mortal. Yet I have kept immortality apart (this double rôle) to greet you. I have kept myself with and away from living. Not sunk, as I was tempted, to that loss of my identity, with Demetrius. A task was imposed on me one night in Athens. Have I completed it?"

Hedyle of Athens was so speaking as to herself, not believing that Demion could sit there. Demion of Olympia was still seated, a little commonplace, a little too heavily static. His head on its thick throat rose like some emperor; his head was heavy, his fibre hardy, his being totally materialized and rock-like.

"If you had been beautiful in the accepted manner, I believe I should have scorned you. You made beauty reality and reality (that was the miracle) sheer beauty.

"You asked me to leave Athens, to go to India. I knew I couldn't do that. I was staring into my own fate, knowing I couldn't do that. Why? One does know these things. Perhaps I loved you too much, was one remove from loving. I was one move off, as if everything I did was done from the reverse side, as if I were moving in a mirror and myself was only a transient reflection of another self that mattered. People could accept the reflection, this Hedyle—" she lifted her arms wanly and the sun caught blue across the blue head of the small snake, "this Hedyle must have had some uncommon power, to project a mirage that would so convince them. I mean, I wanted to convince myself that the mirage forecast the sane reality. If Douris would accept me...the mirage, then the reality, the thing I kept for Demion, must be something worthy. Douris did accept me, has continued doing. If Douris accepted the mirage, dresses and adores it like an image, then the reality must be something worthy. So I proved, have kept proving, to myself my own reality.

"Douris did accept me. He was the highest type of sheer intellectual mortal, without perception that I ever met with. In going away with Douris, I saved my entity. From Demetrius. From Demion. Demion would have gathered me to him as the sun a rain-cloud. Demetrius would have driven me earthward as a marsh sucks in a sluggish river. Douris allowed me my soul's integrity. I was not ready for eternity—"she laughed, blindly seeking words, some utterance that would keep her from muttering, from jibbering, from hysteria. "You know what I mean perfectly."

"You are happy, then, in Samos?"

"Life is climax, anticlimax. I am happy in moments when the sun sets and lies across my lilies, like authentic touch of Demion. I am happy when the stars rise and again when the stars go and dawn says, 'Demion is behind the mountains waiting.' My love for you is linked with an absolute illiterate faith in the materialization, in the reality of beauty. It exists for me in Demion, in the sunlight. I catch Demion in a bird-wing, and sometimes in a dream, he finds me. When Douris embraces me, it is Demion. When my child becomes stern and aloof and secretive, it is his father in him. That is Demion. Demion was the sun and the sun and the sun. To say I loved him would be to cloud a temple-image in a rough cloak. Words as we speak them are as unsuitable to our thought as modern garments to the body. The body in the old days stood naked, so in the old days, no doubt, speech expressed the inexpressible. Our speech no more expresses us than our ungainly garments."

She lifted the ruffled dress stuff. "Still I suppose, as it is getting late, I had really better dress. A blue lily on a dust heap? No, I was only talking. I was so tired. I trust, Demion, you have had a pleasant stay in Samos. I will see the boat off. I presume that you are going. I had not realized you were here or I should sooner have made enquiry for you. Douris is specific in his attention to the foreign delegation and I was sure whoever turned up, would be amply sustained by his provision. I believe someone was to be housed in my old winter-villa. Was it you, Demion?"

He said, "the boy told me you had been there."

"The boy. What boy? O, Hedylus."

"Your son met me on the sea-slope after dinner. He seemed over-stressed and said that he was worried. He sent me to his mother."

"Hedylus?"

"The Athenian."

The Egyptian Cat

THE TURQUOISE-BLUE CAT had caused considerable anxiety. I now keep her wrapped in cotton wool and tissue paper, in a small box within a larger box, stowed away in the back of the case containing my mother's books—those she wrote, and those she read for research and study, or just for fun. That seems as safe a place as any—way off in our secluded country house in eastern Long Island. When I go away she is on her own, and still more secure than she would be with me, travelling back and forth while changing habitats.

I know nothing of her archaeological past, if indeed she has any. H.D. bought her in Egypt in the early 1920's, and brought her home. Genuine artifact, or exquisite facsimile? Experts could tell at a glance. I haven't submitted her to their evaluation, and never will. I don't wish to face up to the responsibility. If she should turn out to be a priceless treasure, I would have to lock her up, or donate her to a museum. Either way—in a bank vault, or in a hall of Egyptology—she would no longer be truly mine. On the other hand, I could never bear to have her diminished. "Sorry, this is just a reproduction." Euphemism for fake. I prefer the mystery.

Genuine or fake, a link with the Pharoahs or merely a souvenir from this century—she is beautiful. She sits inch high, with a proud elongated posture. Her features are finely drawn. They vary—lofty, remote, almost disdainful at times; then tender; then again, inscrutable; always aristocratic. Between her front paws, pressed against her chest, she guards a microscopic replica, her kitten.

Drawing from the occult past, or imitating it, she can behave most unaccountably. She has a life-force of her own.

She came to me in a varied bag of H.D.'s possessions, shortly after her death. It's only by chance that I felt something hard and tiny, tucked deep into the lining.

Then I kept losing her. And she always came back. Burglars ransacked our city home, taking everything, so I thought. Months later, my husband spotted a ridge of turquoise between the floorboards. I carried her around in the zippered compartment of my purse after that. Again, she got away—only to turn up in the back of our stationwagon.

Long, long ago, she hung on a black velvet ribbon around H.D.'s neck. "This is the cat, and this is the kitten," she would say, pointing out the parallel in our relationship.

H.D. was hardly an archetypal mother, nor would one expect her to be. At the time, I really didn't expect or know anything otherwise. We lived in Switzerland with her friend Bryher, isolated from the world. Visitors came by from time to time; mostly writers, adults only. I never consorted with other children, other families, other mothers. So, for all I knew, everybody's mother was a poet; a tall figure of striking beauty, with fine bone structure and haunting grey eyes; and frequently overwrought, off in the clouds, or sequestered in a room, not to be disturbed on any account.

She was intensely maternal—on an esoteric plane. She venerated the concept of motherhood, but was unprepared for its disruptions. She flinched at sudden noise, and fled from chaos. Mercifully for her, she was well-buffered. We had a staff, almost a bodyguard. I could always be removed. *"Madame est nerveuse; viens ma petite!"* Or Bryher would step in and marshal me off. "Your mother's very nervous today." Every day, it seemed. So, fair enough, that's the way it was. A mother was someone who wrote poetry and was very nervous. And who walked alone and sat alone. And was capable of overwhelming affection, but on her own time and terms, preferably out of doors. I accompanied her on her daily walk, clasping a bag full of crusts and crumbs. Always the same time: ten o'clock, when her morning's work was done and put away. The same circuit, down some stone steps to the lake, where we fed the gulls, swans and ducks. Then she reclaimed her solitude. "Run ahead, run, run, *run!*" I charged along and returned, and cantered around her in circles while she strolled and dreamed.

She spent the afternoons in her room, reading, writing letters, and thinking—concentrating on everything and nothing, in an intense trance-like meditation. The Egyptian cat was her mantra. She sat gazing at it for hours, fingering it, running it up and down the velvet ribbon.

When she left the door ajar, I sidled in and joined her. She never objected; she quietly made room for me in the armchair. And I never wriggled, chattered, or wished I were anywhere else. Those were privileged interludes, all the more so for being surreptitious. I dreaded an outsider barging in, breaking up our rapport, our shared secret.

Then I didn't see the little cat, ever again, in my mother's lifetime. Was it already given to disappearing? Or did its presence suddenly become too hypnotic for comfort? At any rate, it was replaced by a crystal which exerted the same psychic pull. I gazed into it, and only saw our reflections, or warped magnifying-glass views of dress and furniture fabric. But she seemed to see something else. If I sat still enough for long enough, I would see too. I stayed absolutely quiet, mesmerized.

Her work—the actual writing—was, of course, a deeply private matter. Then, the door was always closed. She had no workroom as such, only an alcove in her bedroom, stripped down to essentials: a sturdy table, a grey jar full of pencils, a stack of school exercise-books, and a reference book or two. She rose very early, and got straight down to work, filling up the exercise-books with tight faint script. She preferred hard pencils; they lasted longer; she didn't have to interrupt herself with the mechanics of sharpening. When she reached a certain point, she closed all the books and put the pencils back in their jar until next morning.

"Like working on a sampler," she confided, years later. "So many stitches and just so many rows, day after day. If I miss even one day, I drop a stitch and lose the pattern and I feel I'm never going to find it again."

And I ask her about all those other times, when she was not at her desk, yet not entirely in this world—the walks along the lake-front, the sessions with the little cat, with the crystal. Was she dreaming, was she in a sense writing? Well, both; and a correlation of the two.

"Evolving. Searching. My past, the past, the past that never was, and making something real of it. And it's always eluding me. I think I've found it, and I find it's wrong. But the wrong way can be illuminating too, it so often points out the right way—ultimately. The idea *behind* the idea is the one I'm really reaching for. Again, it's a bit like exploring a galaxy with a trick telescope, picking out pin-point constellations, and taking optical illusions for their worth, too. And it's all part of the rag-tag-and-bobtail of my sewing basket. Do you follow me?"

Surprising enough, yes. No matter how dizzying her flights and sudden her descents, or mixed and unexpected her metaphors, I could always follow. I just had to grow up first, and find my own bearings.

She didn't always travel in exalted spheres. Fortunately for her, for me, for her whole *entourage*, she had a marvellous sense of humor; and a spontaneous wit which seized the absurdities of life and everyone's foibles, including her own. So she laughed a lot. The quintessential "loner," nonetheless she loved company. She had many friends, young and old, and some very eminent. Violet Hunt, Elizabeth Bowen, the Sitwells—singly, and triply—Ivy Compton Burnett . . . all came to tea, whenever she was in

London. She was equally interested in people with more humdrum lives. She could involve herself in the daily problems of a veterinarian's assistant—or a typist in a secretarial pool. She mixed all her guests together; being a superb catalyst, everybody had a wonderful time. She also enjoyed ordinary pursuits, jaunts: an afternoon at the movies, bus rides, shopping expeditions. She read current best sellers as well as esoteric tomes. She achieved a perfect balance between anguished sensibility and plain, down-to-earth, everyday life. And, now that the pressures and conflicts of motherhood had ceased, she became a much better mother. We respected each other as individuals. We were adults together, and friends.

And so it is with mothers and daughters, mothers and sons. Another generation has grown up. I've come full circle, with four such friends of my own—who have all played with the Egyptian cat, and admired it.

"But don't worry. Sure you'll lose it again. But it always gets back to you." Possessing an intimate affinity.

Perdita Schaffner

Afterword

FROM THE VERY OPENING, *Hedylus* presents the reader with a world which is formally enclosed—a world structured by the sensibility of its focal *personae,* Hedyle, the mother, and Hedylus, the son. Rather than the broadness of the novel, the book offers the honed depth of poetry. *Hedylus* is *vertical,* hermetic, idiosyncratic; its world encompasses an externalization of inner states. Its shifts in consciousness follow a psychological stream of awareness; its symbols are visualized projections, close to hallucination. Both its main characters are extreme in self-consciousness, *theatrical* in a word; their thoughts form themselves readily into interior monologues, approaching at times the soliloquy of drama. Its exterior events reflect the pattern of their inner world—woven into an intricate network of imagery.

Hedyle and Hedylus are linked together as moon and shadow; as H.D. has written elsewhere (in her *Tribute to Freud*): "One is sometimes the shadow of the other; often one is lost and the one seeks the other. . . ." Or flees the other. For in *Hedylus,* the relationship is more contrast than supplement. One waxes as the other wanes; one lives the other's life, one dies the other's death. *Hedylus* turns on such a death, or rather dying, implying a birth, or rebirth, as well. As Hedylus is born to the present, Hedyle fades from its light into her mirror, her past, herself.

Mirror and bracelet—these symbols are the projected essence of Hedyle. Mirror—self-consciousness, concern for the delineation of appearance, awareness of time and the surface remedy of cosmetics, ornament, ritual formality and acting, posture. The Egyptian lapis bracelet, with the serpent biting its tail—the *ouroboros* (feminine symbol *par excellence*), emblem of death and eternity, transcendence from time, the world of spirit, intact amidst grave-cloths and coffin. The mirror brings the examining glance back to the surface of the skin, upon which the bracelet rests, embracing— at one time in harmony with, and in contrast to, the life pulsing in the blue veins beneath.

For Hedylus, there is the scar on the forehead—the spiritual mark of the god of Delphi, the cleft in his psyche, the trauma of consciousness, the gift of awareness and art. There is also the openness—the ledge above the sea, with a view to sky, sun and stars. This is where he is himself, where through the birth-tunnel of bush and the fall into consciousness, he emerges to declaim his poetry. To meet there Demion, who leads him out of the closed circle of Hedyle. This is his *temenos*; he suffocates within the enclosure of Hedyle's mirror and bracelet. It is Demion who breaks the spell, shatters the glass.

Irene is the contrast to Hedyle; she is the Muse—but it is Demion who brings revelation. Irene—Iris—iridescence. But Demion brings *the god*. Foretold to the pregnant Hedyle when she encounters the snake upon the sun-baked rock, Apollo visits her to make her his own—temple prostitute, prophetess, goddess. Her son will be another Sophocles, or Alexander. While Irene awakens poetry, Demion enables action, self-determination, self-realization.

Hedyle is eminently *the Athenian*; she is blithe, cultivated, refined. But beneath the refinement is weariness. Athens is of the past; she is now on Samos and it was long ago. Vitality is on the wane. Against this, Irene brings the vigor of Nature; her crudity is recognized by Hedylus as also a type of perfection. She gives hope that the pall of ornament and weariness fallen upon Hedylus is premature.

The linkage of Hedylus-Hedyle threatens his life; as in the Taoist symbol of united opposites, the more light absorbed by Hedyle, the less vital impulse remains to him. Demion cuts the umbilical rope with decision. Athens is the already formed world; it belongs to Athene and Apollo. Demion offers to Hedylus the world of Dionysus: to follow the exotic route of Alexander to India; to explore, to go further than the known. To find expression; to be reborn. The butterfly sprouting wings, leaving the chrysalis stage to hover over the dead cocoon. It is only in the unknown that Hedylus can discover himself—outside the shadow of Hedyle.

For Hedyle, Demion has come again "too late," for now her spirit travels through the past. Memory, half-light— neither wholly alive, nor wholly dead. Unilluminated; dying her life, living her death. Apparitions, phantoms flit in the mirror—unrecognized by Hedyle, the Athenian, valuing control and stature, denying the *daemon* under a veneer of elegant fatigue. But passion is there, and flares. However, it is Hedylus who is granted the direct experience—that of the mystery of "living water," the hierophany. The Egyptian bloom promised by the bracelet is fulfilled in him. Hedyle remains frozen on Samos, a statue, a work of art, a beautiful, defined woman—but truncated in time, a stranger to the present. Hedylus' is the impulse to reach beyond—to "the materialization in the reality of beauty" of spirit.

In *Hedylus* the fire of H.D.'s quest for the *numinous* burns with the purity and clarity of her poetry. She delves and returns; themes begun in her poetry, and which appear in her first novel, *Palimpsest* (1922), flicker throughout—to culminate later in the focused light of *Helen in Egypt, Hermetic*

Definition and *Trilogy*. There is no division in the artist H.D.; her prose and poetry are one. The utterance in *Hedylus* coheres with the same intense precision as wrought in her poetry. Phrases and images—fire and ice, blue star, water lilies, flash of gull wing—wind and wend their way throughout the skein of the book; their quasi-musical repetition concentrates, *intensifies*, almost to the point of obsession. The texture tightens with each turn of the loom; the structure stands clear.

Hedylus concerns a search for both identity and transcendence. Hedylus encounters self and godhead at one moment; Hedyle, consciously following the paths of self, misses the turning when the god draws near. Forgetfulness of self and a willingness for death bring Hedylus to himself; the paradox of hermetic turning, the spiral as route to the center. Divinity who eludes direct pursuit, but can be glimpsed as a sheen of light upon the water. To the alchemical awareness of H.D., scattered moments grant hints, as physical details become archetypal traces, signatures of mystery.

Note on the Text

THE PRESENT TEXT OF *HEDYLUS* differs primarily in two regards from that published in 1928 by Basil Blackwell in Oxford (and in America by Houghton Mifflin of Boston): this edition adheres to the paragraphing indicated by H.D. in both typescript and galley proofs (*Paragraphs & conversasations—arrange as in former scripts*, reads H.D.'s note), and encompasses revisions made by H.D. in a notebook kept between January 1951 and May 1953 while she was rereading and rethinking *Hedylus*. [This notebook, blue, measuring 4 5/16" by 6 14/16", and stamped *Cartoleria GARBANI Lugano*, is in the Collection of American Literature, Beinecke Rare Book and Manuscript Library, Yale University—whose curator, Donald Gallup, and staff are to be thanked for their help and cooperation.] Both H.D.'s grammatical punctuations, as idiosyncratic as they might appear at first glance, and spelling (with its fondness for hyphenation), for the most part, have been followed throughout as indications of both sequence and emphasis of thought, and flow of utterance, since H.D. is primarily a poet, even while writing prose—her statements cohere rhythmically, imagistically and dramatically. As in poetry, the placement of words upon a page in *Hedylus* has both a calligraphic and ideogrammatic significance; thus the original paragraphing, by opening out both verbal image and visual design, elucidates and isolates.

The following section, *Images*, reproduces the words, phrases and images that H.D. had singled out and marked in her notebook *(described above)*; these not only serve as the structural nexus of imagery for *Hedylus*, but echo throughout her later work. Perhaps reverberating in her mind while meditating on the earlier appearance of images of such enduring, poignant significance, the inner continuity of symbolism becomes apparent. In her notebook, H.D. drew out from the texture of prose truncated revelations, haunting, disembodied phrases . . . evocative, enigmatic, emblematic. Workpoints for the novel; living symbols for the poet.

IMAGES

p. 7	Only there is no time.
p. 12	iridescent *(dic. coloured like iris or rainbow)—O Paphian.*
p. 14	. . . a ghost summoned—*(Hedylus)—*
p. 15	a ghost regarded a painted image . . . winter-pavilion.
pp. 20-1	gash—psychically blighted
p. 21	the child of a goddess.
p. 23	She saw in him . . . herself
p. 25	Irene—Muse
p. 26	She didn't ask for pity, not even understanding.
p. 26	Under the winter-blossoms the winter blossoms
p. 27	stones like icy little knuckles
p. 29	He cared too much for writing.
p. 30	to find his own God. Her very name (his very name) upset him.
p. 31	washed finally seaward a live blue star *(Hedyle)*

p. 33   love-child of an Athenian

p. 34   I am a bastard—the court of beauty.

p. 34   cyclamen . . . like a red-star . . .

p. 35   protective deity
          . . . his protective deity (*Artemis*)

p. 37   Irene . . . blue-star.

p. 39   through some catastrophe-stricken wall.
          winter-poppies ⟨appears twice, ed.⟩
          psychic-wound ⟨appears twice, ed.⟩

p. 40   death-wound.
          faced reality [*Irene*]

p. 41   Something . . . was already set in order.

p. 43   Muse—mother—sister

p. 44   Irene . . . visual magnet
          sort of visual magnet

pp. 45-6   . . . bush-tunnel [*birth-symbol.*]
          bush tunnel
          hypnotized

p. 46   tense visionary moments of fulfilment
          hands praying, as on some archaistic altar.

p. 47   Iridescent . . . Thetis ⟨appears twice, ed.⟩ [*sea, mother,*
          birth, death symbols to Hedylus]—silver water [*silver*
          mirror of Hedylus]—
          frozen dream-state.
          . . . his frozen dream-state

p. 47   some god maybe ⟨appears twice, ed.⟩ [*his father*]

p. 54   pure thought . . . iridescence like transient rainbow
          his tired head

p. 55   a sort of invocation
          . . . invocation [*poems*]

pp. 56-7   . . . invoking daemons.
          She died, I am sure, in Athens.
          Irene hasn't been born yet, Hedyle is *dead already.* ⟨the
          latter forcefully underscored, ed.⟩

154

156

BLACK SWAN BOOKS
Literary Series

☐ H. D., *Hedylus*

☐ CARLOS DRUMMOND DE ANDRADE,
The Minus Sign

☐ LAWRENCE DURRELL, *The Ikons*

☐ EZRA POUND/JOHN THEOBALD, *Letters*

☐ PETER JONES, *The Garden End*

☐ *Three Fates in Taos*

☐ ADRIAN STOKES, *With All the Views*

☐ VERNON WATKINS, *Unity of the Stream*

Catalogue available

Published by
BLACK SWAN BOOKS LTD.
P. O. BOX 327
REDDING RIDGE, CT 06876